Hallow'eve™ Frights – Book 1

ALL THE KIDS LOVE THAT SCARY STUFF

Story By

Bibly O'Grim

Book By

Randy Moses

Copyright © 2015 Randy Moses

All Rights Reserved

LEGAL NOTES

No part of this book may be reproduced, scanned, or distributed in any printed or electronic form known, or unknown, without permission from the author. Please do not participate in, or encourage, the piracy of copyrighted materials in violation of the author's rights.

Thank you for respecting the hard work of this author.

This is a work of fiction. Names, characters, places, and incidents either are the product of the author's imagination or are used in a fictitious manner. Any resemblance to locations, events, establishments, or actual persons – living, dead, or undead – is entirely coincidental.

Author's Content Advisory

All The Kids Love That Scary Stuff contains no foul language, nor violence. As a Halloween story, it does feature some scary events, however I believe it is suitable for the entire family, except perhaps for the most sensitive of very young children (or parents).

Kind regards.

Author's Format Advisory

Please note that the author takes artistic liberties with many of the standard formatting conventions of literature and grammar. He does this to help better express his ideas to the reader. Thank you for understanding.

Table of Contents

Introduction 5

7:23am – Goodrich House 9

10:06am – 1717 Fleet St. 12

10:38am – Grover Creek 16

11:23am – Main St. 25

12:01pm – Carolina Cinema 39

2:22pm – Town Square. 65

3:56pm – 1713 Fleet St. 69

4:03pm – Town Square 73

5:17pm – Town Square. 86

5:56pm – Town Square. 98

6:32pm – 1713 Fleet St. 105

6:40pm – Town Square. 114

6:46pm – Town Square. 118

6:51pm – Goodrich House. 123

6:55pm – Town Square. 127

6:55pm – Old Mill Rd. 129

6:55pm – Goodrich House. 129

7:09pm – Main St. 136

About The Authors 146

INTRODUCTION

I was a small boy when I first met *Bibly O'Grim*. It was on Halloween Night, and I was out trick-or-treating. That year, to the best of my recollection, I was dressed in a Ben Cooper *Superman* costume. I recall that it had no sleeves, so my mother dressed me in a long sleeved shirt, and stuffed towels in the arms for faux bicep muscles. Moms are clever that way.

Although I had started out by myself, I quickly congregated with a random group of other trick-or-treaters, going door to door. Which was common practice at the time. It didn't matter so much if you knew *who* you were trick-or-treating with, as it did if you knew who they were *dressed* as.

As the evening wore on, you'd lose a bit of your group at a time, as their parents told them it was "time to go." So, you'd say goodbye to your makeshift *Candy Brigade* in the only way you knew how: "Goodbye, Frankenstein!" "Goodbye, Buck Rogers!" "Good-bye, Mork!" "Got any extra bubble-gum?"

The group had dwindled down to just two before my mom told me it was time to go. I turned to my last remaining Brigade member, a bedsheet ghost, and wished him good-bye:

"Bye, Scary Ghost!"

"Can I have your caramel apple?" he asked me, in a rather peculiar voice.

I looked down into my bag and saw what appeared to be a caramel apple, wrapped in paper. I didn't recall receiving it. A quick glance at the old pillowcase he was using as a candy bag, showed me he didn't have a very good haul this year. I took the apple out of my bag, and dropped it into his.

"Good lad!" he said.

My mom and I returned to my grandparents' house, who we were staying with at the time. I took my candy bag, and headed straight out to the backyard. My grandparents had a big concrete porch in the back, and I was allowed out there, as long as I didn't leave the yard.

I flew around the backyard, cape flapping in the wind. I leaped over tall bushes in a single bound, and bent the garden hose with my bare hands. I was standing on the concrete picnic table when I saw a rather short bedsheet ghost standing in the yard. I was immediately sure it was the same one as before.

"Hello!" I called to him.

"Hello Lad! I was on my merry way, when I realized that I should have offered to share the apple with you."

He walked over and joined me at the picnic table. He placed his pillowcase down flat, and laid the apple on top of it. Removing his bedsheet costume, he revealed himself not to be a child, but... what I will refer to as *a little person*.

He had shoulder-length shaggy red hair, a full red beard, a kind smiling face, and a twinkle in his eye. His ears came to a slight point. For some reason, he reminded me of Santa Claus.

"Bibly O'Grim is my name, and storytelling is my game," he said, splitting the apple with a pocket-knife. "Here lad. Here's your share. As I always say: 'Hallow'eve is for friends!'"

Hallow'eve... he always calls it that.

"Now, my boy, as we sit here and enjoy our evening's bounty, let me regale you with a story of Hallow'eve Past. Yes, I remember it like it was just yesterday..."

He then went on to tell me an incredible tale, one of a pumpkin buccaneer, a flying pirate ship, strange little imps, and an invasion of New York City! I was spellbound by his story. (I've got to get around to writing a book about that one some time.)

When he had finished his tale, he stood up and said:

"Well, that's all for one night, young man. I've got much more to do on this night of nights. But, if you mind your manners, and leave a nice hot cup of tea out back, next Hallow'eve, for good ol' Bibly, I might just drop by with another tale to tell."

Every year, I minded my manners. Every year, I left a cup of hot tea out back for him. Every year, he visited.

I didn't always get to *see* him, but I always knew he had stopped by, because the tea was always gone from the cup the next morning, and in its place, he always left me a piece of candy as a 'thanks.'

When I do get to see Bibly, he often wears a different costume, and always spins a different yarn about the wonders, and secrets, of *Hallow'eve*. He has never run out of fantastic stories, and I don't think he ever will…

On the Halloween before I began writing this very book, as we sat on my back porch sipping hot tea, and taking turns at *Cornhole*, I casually asked Bibly if he would mind if I wrote a book or two about the many stories he has told me over the years. He blinked at me, a bit in wonder, and replied:

"Are ya daft? Why do ya' think I've been telling ya' them?"

And so… here I am typing the introduction to book one.

I hope you have as much fun reading it, as I had writing it. It's an exciting Halloween tale suited for young and old alike. Kids will love the scary adventure, while adults will love the nostalgia.

Enjoy!

-Randy

DEDICATION

For

Anna

7:23AM – GOODRICH HOUSE

SATURDAY OCTOBER 31ST, 1981

The Carolina wind whistled a ghostly tune.

Harriet Angela Goodrich stepped out of her backdoor, laundry basket in hand, and walked to the maze of clothes lines that crowded her backyard. Placing the basket on an old stump, she pulled each item out, one at a time, and began hanging them very neatly out to dry. She had opted to use the more modern spring loaded clothes pins for laundry, as they were only linens and towels. When she hung her garments out, she typically used the old fashioned style hangers, with the round heads at the top. In her experience these were less likely to leave impressions on clothing than the newer version. Pin marks on a towel did not bother her, but she disdained them on a blouse. Years of experience made the chore quick, simple, and efficient. After completing the task, she picked up her basket, glanced at her watch, and marched back inside.

A moment later, she re-emerged from her home, but this time, out the front door, with her arms wrapped around a cardboard box. She stepped to the edge of her porch, placed the box down, and stood quietly, glancing once more at her watch.

"Time and tide, Mr. Porter. Time and tide," she said to herself.

After another full minute, Harriet saw the old heap that was Edgar William Porter's 1951 Ford F1 Pickup come around the corner. It knocked, clanked, and groaned as it came to a sputtering stop at the end of her walkway. It was yet one minute more before the man himself made his way out the door, and started up the path. He waved at her.

"Good morning, Harriet!"

"Good morning, Edgar."

"I'm a bit late."

"Not terribly so. I've always thought that a person should be allowed one extra minute, for every year they are over thirty, before they can be considered late."

"If I had known that," he said, stopping at the porch steps, "I would have slept in a bit."

Harriet raised an eyebrow at him

"If you had done that, I would have come and dragged you out of bed myself."

Edgar wiped his brow, and eyed the box on the porch.

"Those the candles?"

"Five dozen. Give or take."

"The Holiday Committee appreciates you donating them, Harriet."

"Thank my sister, Hedy. Her and her bees. She has more wax than she knows what to do with. So, I end up having more candles than I know what to do with."

Edgar placed his left foot on the top step, reached down, and pushed the box flaps apart. He pulled a single candle out and inspected it. The wax felt slippery in his hand.

"Can't remember the last time I held one of these. It's a bit of a lost art."

"Our mother taught both Hedy and me how to make them. She was a firm believer in the old ways."

"Thank goodness for that." Edgar said, returning the candle to the box. He then picked up the box and rested it on his knee. "You can't have a proper Jack-o-lantern without a good candle."

"The store bought ones never seem to burn as long. I think they make them that way, so you have to buy more."

Edgar smiled.

"You sure I can't change your mind about coming to the carving contest tonight, Harriet?"

"No. If I did that, who'd be here when the children come knocking?"

"If you change your mind, we'd love to have you."

"I'll consider it," Harriet chimed. "Now go on, if you're going to be on time to meet Jake Tallman."

"Jake's not bringing the pumpkins in until a bit later. But I do need to go help Mrs. Sutter set up at town square."

"You be sure to give Margie my best wishes."

"Will do."

Edgar Porter turned, and walked down the path towards his Ford, taking the time to eye the manner of decorations Harriet had in her yard. They were mostly variations on scarecrows. Some had pumpkin heads, others just white burlap hoods with eyeholes cut out. She even had hung a few old bedsheets from her two trees to look like ghosts. He knew Harriet never went in for all the store brand decorations this time of year, and he admired her for that.

When he reached his truck, he placed the box in the cargo bed. He turned back to wave bye to Harriet, but she must have already gone inside. Edgar climbed into the cab, started up the engine, and after a moment of letting it warm up, drove off.

10:06AM – 1717 FLEET ST.

Rob Hanson was having a major dilemma. He flipped through the *Montgomery Ward Christmas Catalog,* and once again turned to the page he had dog-eared. Page 469.

What to get?

What to get?

What to get?

He already had item "K". So, there was no need for another one. His parents said that "F" was too expensive. Item "L" looked kind of dumb. That left him with a choice between item "M" and item "G." Sure, "M" lighted up, but "G" just seemed so much cooler.

Lost in thought, he was about to finish his second bowl of Fruit Brute, when Rick Davenport knocked on his door. He knew it was Rick by the four quick, hard raps.

"Come on Rob!"

Knock. Knock. Knock. Knock.

"Rob, come on out!"

Rob rolled his eyes, placed his bowl back on his TV tray, got up from his quilt palette in front of the living room television, and walked toward the door.

"Hold your horses, Rick."

"Come on, Rob."

Knock. Knock. Knock. Knock.

"Don't knock so hard, or you'll make my parents mad."

Rob turned the latch on the deadbolt, and opened the door. He stared at Rick through the screen door. He liked Rick. He just wished Rick would grow-up some. But what could he expect from a guy who still watched *Sesame Street?*

"What is it?"

"Jason Meadows is out by Grover Creek," Rick said excitedly, flailing his hands about. "He's going to try to jump it. The whole gang is down there."

"So?"

"So?!' He asked with genuine surprise. "So, you've got to come watch him!"

"No way."

"Why not?"

"Look, *Kids Super Power Hour* is still on. Then comes *Spider-Man.* If I leave now, I'll not only miss both of them, but I'll miss *Blackstar* as well." With conviction he added: "And you know I'm not missing *Blackstar*."

"*Blackstar* will always be on later," Rick argued. "You don't want to be the only one in class on Monday morning not to have seen Jason jump it!"

"Keep it down, my brother's still asleep, ok?" Rob opened the screen door and stepped outside, closing the main door behind him. "He ain't gonna make the jump anyhow."

"You don't know that! His dad just got him a new BMX Mongoose for his birthday. It's brand new! That means it's fast."

"Umm."

"Craig is going to meet us down there. He told me to get you."

"Umm."

"Come on, I don't want to miss it."

Rob pushed the main door open, stuck his head in, and called out:

"Mom, Dad, I'm going with Rick down to the creek!"

"Take your jacket, honey," his mother's voice answered in reply.

Rob looked back at Rick.

"Hold on."

Rob stepped back into his home and closed the door shut behind him. He hurried to the hall closet and fished out his denim jacket. Slipping it on, he walked back to the door. On the hall table he spotted a small stack of quarters. He studied them for a moment. Then shrugged, and scooped them up into his jacket pocket.

Another voice came from the kitchen.

"Hey son, be back before five, or no trick-or-treating!"

"Ok, dad."

With that, Rob stepped outside, and pulled the door shut behind him.

In the kitchen, Rob's mother called over to her husband.

"Jeff, I need to talk to you."

"What about, hon?" he asked.

Amanda Hanson finished pouring her coffee, walked across the kitchen floor, and joined him at the breakfast table. Jeff was eating a bowl of Banana Frosted Flakes, along with two pieces of toast, and a large glass of orange juice. She sipped her coffee and warmed her hands with the mug.

"I'm worried about Rob," she said.

"Worried about what?" he said, looking up at her.

"He reads that *Ghosts* comic. Has that *Frankenstein* poster on his wall. Last night he sat in the living room with you and watched that entire horror movie on television. I'm just wondering if he should be into all that scary stuff at his age."

"Oh that?" He laughed a bit and smiled at his wife. "There's nothing wrong with that. We let Paul watch *The Exorcist* when it was on TV back in May, and it didn't bother him any."

"Paul is older."

"Just a few years."

"But that can make a difference."

"Honey," Jeff put his spoon down by the side of his bowl and leaned in toward his wife. "The world can be a scary place. I don't like that, but it's the truth. We don't do our children any good by sheltering them too much. Besides, they're just stories."

"But is it normal?"

"Sure, when I was his age I loved to watch all those movies with Bela Lugosi and Boris Karloff. They're fun for kids. Also, in a way, I think it helps them face the fears of growing up."

"Really?"

"Really. There's nothing to worry about." Jeff reached across the table and gently pushed the hair out of his wife's face. "Besides, these days, *all* the kids love that 'scary stuff'."

10:38AM – GROVER CREEK

"What are we still waiting for?!"

"I told you. Rick and Rob are still coming. "

"They need to hurry up, Craig."

"What's your big hurry, Billy?"

    "Yeah!"   "What?"

"I have to go up to old lady Goodrich's in a couple of hours, and rake her yard and stuff."

"Why you doing that?"

"My dad told her I would. He says I need it to build character."

"So, what did you do this time?"

"None of your bee's wax, Craig."

"You track dog poop on your mom's carpet again?"

    "Ha-ha"

    "Hee-hee-hee."

    "I bet."

"She spank you again?"

"None of your bee's wax, Craig."

"Did it hurt?"

    Ha!"   "Oooh."

    "Ouch."

"I said, none of your bee's wax!"

"Back off, Billy."

"Yeah, back off."

"You watch it, Meadows!"

"Or?

"Or you'll be jumping over that creek with a fat lip."

"Why, you going to punch him through me?"

"Maybe I will."

"Maybe you won't."

"Who's gonna stop me?"

"Me."

"Him."

"Hey Rob, about time."

"You startin' something, Weaks?"

"More like Craig and Meadows are."

"No way, we were just waiting on you and Rick."

"Look, is he going to jump this or not?"

"Yeah, I am."

"So let's do it."

"Ok."

"Alright."   *"Finally!"*

"Yeah."   *"About time!"*

"Ok Meadows, you start up there, come down the hill, and go over the plank. It's easy."

"If it's easy, why don't you do it?"

"I already did."

"Huh?" "Whaa?"

"You did not."

"Did so, I was here last Sunday morning with Jack Porter, and he saw me do it."

"Uh-uh."

"Naaw." *"No way"*

"You can ask him on Monday."

"Don't worry, I can do it."

"Jason, just remember when you take off, keep pedaling. If you keep pedaling, you'll jump further."

"Oh Rick, you do not!"

"Yes, you do. Everyone knows that."

"I don't see how."

"You just do."

"Rob, will you help me carry my bike up?"

"Yeah."

"Thanks."

"Ok, I'll say 'go.'"

"No, I will."

"Why you?"

"Cause I jumped it before. So I say 'go' now. When someone else jumps it, then they can say 'go.'"

"But you didn't jump it."

"You calling me a liar?"

"Yes."

   "Uh-oh."

   "Oooooooooh…."

"If you did it before Billy, why don't you do it again?'

"Uh…"

"You can go next."

"I did it, I don't have to do it again."

"Sez you."

"Hey guys, I'm ready!"

"Ok Meadows!"

"You show him, Meadows."

"I'll try.'

"Ready?"

"I said I'm ready."

   "Right."

"On your mark, get set… *slow!*"

"Come on, Billy."

   "Yeah."

   "Quit that."

"On your mark, get set… *flow!*"

"You're such a dope."

"Ha."

"Yeah, dope."

"Quit."

"Alright. On you mark, get set…*GO!*"

"*Go Meadows!*" "*Yeah!*"

"*You can do it!*"

"*Look at him go!*"

"WOOoooOO!"

"Go!"

"Go!!"

"Go!!!"

"*Wooooot!*"

"Yeah!

"*Wooooot!!*"

"Go, Jason!"

"Burn it, Meadows*!*"

"*Do it!*"

"*Wooooot!!!*"

"*Here he goes!!*"

"Take off!"

"*Yes!*"

"Keep pedaling!"

"*Woo-hoo!*"

20

"Aaaaaaaaaaaaaaaaaaaa

a

a

a

a

a

g

h

h

!"

"OOOFFF!!!"

"Uh-oh!!"   *"Yikes!"*

"Whoa!"   *"Ouch!!"*

"Help him up! Help him up!"

"Oh, man!"

"Is he ok?"

"Help him up! Help him up!"

"That's gotta hurt!"

"See, I told you so."

"Meadows!"

"You Ok, Meadows?"

"Yeah, I'm ok. Just wet."

"See? You didn't even get halfway."

"Let him alone, Billy!"

"My mom's gonna kill me."

"Well, I told you to keep pedaling."

10:55am – Town Square

Margie Sutter had just finished setting up the last folding chair when Jake Tallman drove up in his red and white 1970 Chevrolet C-10. Margie looked up, smiled and regarded him with approval. She liked Jake a great deal. He was an abundantly happy man with an infectious smile. Margie called out to Edgar Porter, who was hammering on the pavilion roof.

"Ed. Jake is here. Come down and lend him a hand."

"On my way," said Ed Porter, climbing down his ladder. "How do the pumpkins look?"

"Can't tell yet."

Jake drove his vehicle to a stop and hopped out. He put his ball cap back on and waved to his two friends. He approached Margie and gave her a friendly hug.

"How you doing Margie?" Jake inquired in his usual energetic way.

"Good Jake, good. You?"

"Well, I didn't see my name in the obituaries this morning. So, I reckon I ain't doing too bad!" He said, laughing as he slapped his knee.

"Well, when you get up one morning, and do see it there, be sure to give me a call."

"You'll be the first."

Ed made his way over to the truck and joined them.

"What took you so long today Jake? You wouldn't tell me this morning on the phone," he asked.

"I had me one heck of a great idea. So great, I had to drive out to Russ Martin's hardware store right away," Jake replied.

"That's a long way to go so early in the morning. What was it?"

Jake took Margie by the hand and eagerly led her to the back of his truck.

"Do you remember last year when little Derek Winters brought his own pumpkin to the carving contest?"

"Oh yes," Margie said touching her hand to her cheek. "Derek Sr. had painted it with that bright orange spray paint which he uses to mark his firewood trees with."

"Yes, 'fluorescent' it's called," pulling down the tailgate on his flat bed, revealing a large cardboard box.

"Anyway," Margie continued, "all the kids just loved the way it looked. All bright and shiny. It was a big hit. I know my Charlie talked about it all week."

"Last night, I got the notion that it would be a treat for all the kids in town to have pumpkins like that for carving. So, I called old Russ up this morning, drove all the way out there, and looky here!"

Jake opened the box and produced two cans of Krylon fluorescent spray paint.

"Russ donated a whole box of that there paint, in different colors. There's orange cans, red cans, yellow, and green. We're going to paint all the pumpkins with them."

"Fine idea Jake," Ed chimed in.

"Then, when the kids are done carving them, we'll display them all under the pavilion, like we always do. But we'll replace the pavilion's regular light bulbs, with these here UV ones that Russ gave me. When the kids are all gathered around, we'll flip the switch, and all the little one's Jack-o-lanterns will light up like the moon!"

"Oh, I cannot wait to see the look on their faces," Margie said, clapping her hands together.

"Me either."

"Jake, if we are going to get these all painted, we had better start with the unloading," said Ed.

"Right-o."

"I'll lay down the morning newspaper, so we can start painting," Margie added, heading toward her car.

Jake and Ed began unloading the pumpkins from the back of the Chevy, placing them underneath the pavilion. After a moment Margie returned from the car with the newspaper, and began spreading it out on the ground, using rocks for weight. She started selecting pumpkins from the pavilion, and placed them on the newspaper. She was quite pleasantly surprised by how big they were. There didn't appear to be a runt in the whole lot.

"Jake, this must be the finest bunch of pumpkins I've ever seen."

"You can thank Harriet for that," Jake said, continuing to unload the truck. "She gave me some of that special 'plant juice' her momma taught her to make. The whole patch is bursting with the plumpest pumpkins I've ever grown."

"Then you better save me a couple for Thanksgiving."

"I will. I will. You want me to save you one too, Ed?"

"No, I think I'll be fine."

"Let me know if you change your mind. Margie, why don't you start painting them while we finish unloading. Here!" Jake reached in to the box, and grabbed a can of bright fluorescent green paint, and tossed it at her. "Start with this one."

Margie caught the can, and began shaking it up. She walked over to the first pumpkin on the paper, and pressed the nozzle down. A stream of bright green paint shot out. Effortlessly, she began coating the pumpkin with it.

11:23AM – MAIN ST.

Rick Davenport was the proud owner of his dad's 1956 Schwinn Phantom bicycle, and it was a beauty. Red with black trim, the *Phantom* featured a chrome trimmed tank and chrome fenders. It had a spring fork, and a leather seat. To top it all off, there was a built-in fender light and an electric horn. He had added the brand new streamers himself.

His granddad had entrusted Rick with its upkeep, and Rick had really pulled through. He polished the chrome every day, and kept the seat supple with saddle soap. If it was going to rain, he would cover the bike with a tarp. The chain was always oiled, and the white wall tires seemed to glow. It made them both proud.

Robert Hanson loved his 1978 Sears Screamer MX. The *Screamer* was an off-the-road motocross bike designed for dirt track riding, sporting a simple single speed gear with rear coaster brakes. It featured a bright yellow wedge style steel frame, with an extra strong flat girder fork, and sturdy handlebars for rugged riding. It had wide black knobby tires with heavy-duty chrome rims and spokes. The chain guard had the words "free spirit" printed on it.

It had been a hand-me-down from his brother Blake, but Rob didn't care. A good bike was a good bike. Although he kept the tires inflated, and the chain oiled, he didn't go for all that "spit and polish" stuff like everyone else. A bike like this was meant to be ridden, not looked at. Besides, it was his now, and he was going to ride it into the ground if he wanted to.

Craig Chambers loved his 1980 Raleigh Chopper MK2. The *Chopper* was a highly stylized bike, designed to resemble a chopper motorcycle, by having a front tire that was smaller than the rear one. Its frame was a slick black with silver lettering. It had silver "ape hanger" handlebars, and a long black seat with a high back. The chain guard had a picture of a hot rod engine blowing fire out of the back. His favorite part was the five speed derailleur gears, operated by the bright red T-Bar lever mounted to the frame.

The Chopper had been a birthday present from his dad. Craig was thrilled to get it, and used the garden hose to keep it fairly clean, especially the seat. He loved riding it up and down the street, popping wheelies and jumping makeshift ramps. He even invented a sport, where he would ride it around the driveway, trying to shoot a basketball into the hoop over the garage. Wicked cool.

The three friends rode in unison up Main St. toward Town Square. As they approached the town's center, Rob called to the other two:

"Come on! We gotta go the 7-Eleven!"

"Why?" asked Rick.

"I thought we said we were going to the theater to play *Black Knight*?"

26

"Paul told me they got a new game at the 7-Eleven in on Wednesday. We've gotta check it out."

"I already played their new game. It came in the Wednesday before," countered Craig.

"That was the other one. He says this one is brand new, and the coolest game ever."

"I thought the other one was pretty cool."

"Naw, it's too much like *Defender*, and I hate *Defender*."

"*Defender's* too hard. You can only play about ten seconds before your ship's destroyed," agreed Rick.

"Well, what's the new one called?"

"I don't remember. Blake said it's cool because the whole thing just looks like glowing outlines in space, and you shoot a lot."

"You got any quarters?'

"Yeah, I got extra, plus my allowance."

"Mr. West will give you change if you ask him nicely," said Rick.

"As long as he has quarters in the register, last time he didn't."

"Hey, look over there," said Craig, as he put on his brakes. The other boys stopped in suit. Craig pointed over to the Town Square pavilion. "It looks like they're setting up for tonight."

"I wonder if they're giving out any candy tonight?" asked Rob.

"Yep. My mom and dad are helping out later. They picked up a lot of candy for it. They said Mrs. Sutter is making fresh caramel for the apples," Craig offered in reply.

"Neat," said Rick. "When's it start?"

"About 5:00pm."

"I'll have to check it out. Now, can we go to 7-Eleven already?"

"What's your problem, Rob?'

"I'm hungry."

"You're always hungry."

"Am not!"

"Are too," Craig parroted back.

"Am not."

"Are too."

"Will you quit?!" Rob said folding his arms.

"Relax, just yanking your chain," Craig chuckled, and shook his head. "C'mon, let's go."

With that, the boys continued on their bikes, down the street to the 7-Eleven.

11:32am – Mr. West's Store.

Rob burst into the store, followed by Craig, then Rick. They called to the man behind the counter as they passed him:

"Morning!"

"Good morning, Mr. West!"

"Good morning, sir!"

"Good morning, boys! Good morning, Rick!" Mr. West responded with a friendly wave.

The trio headed straight into the back of the store, where the arcade cabinets where kept. There were three machines now in total. On the far right was *Stargate*. In the middle was *Donkey Kong*. On the left was the new game, housed in a shiny cabinet of blues, reds and bright purples. The artwork across the top showed strange otherworldly beasties reaching out from a mysterious red ether. Looking at the screen, the boys saw the title streaking out of the black background, into the front, in a trail of blue, red, purple and white letters. Finally, the title was left floating center screen in bright white. It was an impressive sight.

"Wow," Craig stated simply.

"*Tempest*," said Rob in awe, lifting his hands in front of him, as if framing the words for emphasis.

"It has vector graphics, in color!"

"I don't even know what that means, Rick," remarked Craig.

"It means the graphics look like they're drawn on the screen, like *Asteroids* is."

"I'm playing first!" called Rob.

"Why you?"

"Because it was my idea, and I called it," Rob replied in triumph.

"Then just play already, Rob."

"Nothing doing. I'm gonna get me one of those large ham and cheeses with a Big Gulp first."

"Rob!"

"Just wait."

Rob strolled over to the refrigerated section, leaving his friends behind.

"While he's doing that, I'm going to go check-out their cards."

"Ok," said Craig as he examined the instructions on the game's cabinet.

Rob opened the refrigerator door and grabbed a big hoagie-style ham and cheese sandwich. He walked over to the fountain drink dispenser and pulled down a red Big Gulp paper cup from the dispenser. He looked over at the Slurpee machine and called to Craig.

"Hey Craig, do you need this MLB cup?"

"Which one is it?"

"The *Atlanta Braves*."

"Nope, I got that one."

"Ok."

Rob placed his cup up against the machine and dispensed ice into it until filled to the top. He then eyed the various soft drink choices dubiously.

"What drink should I get?"

It was Rick he heard in reply.

"Get a rainbow burster."

'What's that?"

"That's when you get a little of every kind," Rick replied incredulously. "Everyone knows that."

"Oh."

Rob then began to systematically fill his cup from each of the nozzles a little at a time. He over filled slightly on the last one,

30

and had to sip it down in order to snap the plastic lid on. He stuck a long straw in the top, picked the whole thing up in his arms, and then proceeded toward the register. When he arrived, he found Mr. West absent, so he gave the service bell two quick rings.

Meanwhile, Rick was over in the candy aisle, slowly scanning the top shelf for trading cards.

Let's see.

    Football?

No.

    Baseball?

No.

    Dallas?

Definitely not!

    Dallas Cowboy Cheerleaders?

Why?

    Raiders?

Sold out!

    Ms. Pac-Man?

Dumb stickers.

    Magnum P.I.?

Shouldn't be on at the same time as Mork & Mindy.

Ah!

Rick's attention turned to the single pack of *The Dukes of Hazzard* trading cards left in the box.

Yee-haw!

He reached his hand over to get it, when someone snatched it up from under him.

"Aw, too bad, so sad!"

It was Tanner Blake, know it all, and a fourteen year old bully. Tanner was accompanied by his fellow purveyor of ill fortune, Terri Driscoe. Tanner held the card pack up to his face, and wallowed in mock sorrow.

"Were you going to get this?"

"Give it back, Tanner."

"Back? You never had it to start with."

"You took it just before I did."

"I got to it first, and I'm buying it."

"That's not fair, Tanner."

"Seems fair to me," Driscoe said, laughing with Tanner in unison.

"You're just a bully, Tanner."

"So? What are you going to do about it?"

Rick stood in silence.

"That's what I thought."

Tanner turned and headed to the register. Driscoe followed. Craig came around the corner into the candy aisle.

"You ok, Rick?"

"Yeah. No big deal."

The two returned to the back of the shop, where Rob met up with them. Rob placed his drink on the ground next to the cabinet. He took a bite of his sandwich and placed it on the cabinet's control deck.

"There's no joystick."

"You use this knob to spin your Blaster ship, and this button to fire. The other button is your super-zapper, to destroy everything on screen, but only use it once a level," explained Craig.

"Ok."

Rob put his quarter into the machine and pressed the flashing 'one player' button. He then pressed the fire button to begin. The game sprung to life as the first playing field, a circular tube appeared on the screen. Enemy targets appeared at the far end and started to make their way up the tube, firing destructive bursts of energy as they did. Frantically, Rob spun the controller around and round, hitting the fire button as fast as he could.

"This is hard to control. It just goes around in circles," he cried.

"Turn it slower," Rick said. "Don't just spin it."

"There's a bad guy at the top!"

"What do I do?"

"Hit your super-zap! Hit your super-zap!"

Rob pressed the super-zapper, clearing the stage of enemies. In doing so, he caused the Blaster to 'warp' into the second level.

"That was cool," Craig noted.

"This one's shaped like a square."

"Just keep shooting them. If one gets to the top, zap it again."

Rob struggled to spin around the field and blast his targets away. He got hit by one of the energy balls, and lost his first life. The game started up again, and Rob waged his ship in a battle to survive just the second level. Another well timed super-zap saved the day, and he proceeded to warp again to the third screen. During this time, Tanner and Driscoe walked over and stood behind the kids.

The third screen was shaped like a 'plus' sign, and played just like the previous two. Rob lost his second life to an unnoticed enemy that made its' way topside. He managed to clear the rest of the screen, and moved on to the fourth.

The fourth screen was more of an oval shape, and the enemies moved faster. This time, green swirls came spinning up parts of the field, leaving a green line trialing behind them. Rob didn't know what that meant, but he was too busy to care. Another round of random firing and super-zapping cleared the screen and the field began to warp. But this time two words appeared on the screen that hadn't before: "Avoid Spikes." Rob's ship warped right into one of the green tails that the swirls had left, and was blown-up, ending Rob's game.

"Eight thousand six hundred, fifty-two points," barked Tanner. "You suck!"

"I do not!"

"You couldn't do any better," added Rick.

"I could do better than any of you."

"Wanna bet?" asked Craig.

"What?"

"I bet I can score more points than you can."

"No way."

"Prove it."

"I will."

"But if I win, you have to leave us alone, and give Rick that pack of cards he wanted."

"Ok. If I win, you have to buy me another one, of my choice."

"Deal," Craig said, motioning toward the machine. "You go first."

"I will."

Tanner inserted his coin, pressed the 'one player' button, smirked at Craig, and quickly hit the fire button to start. He carefully made his way around the field, blasting enemies and dodging energy bursts. He effortlessly made his way through the first 3 levels without even using his super-zap. When the fourth level came up, he made sure to destroy the green swirls as fast as he could. He even used his Blaster to destroy some of the green spikes, one piece at a time. He laughed as he surpassed Rob's score.

Tanner made it through screen five as quickly as he did number four. When he reached level six though, the enemies started to come even faster, and almost the entire field had green swirls spinning up it. Nervous, he hit the super-zap button early in the level. It cleared the current targets, but more kept coming. Tanner lost his first ship to an energy blast. The game started up again, and he cleared all the enemies, but lost his second ship to a small green spike while he warped to the seventh level.

Level seven was no easier than the last. He shot down enemies as fast as he could, but they seemed to be everywhere. Two red ones made their way to the top at the same time, and crushed his final ship. His total score was eighteen thousand eight hundred fifty-six. In triumph, he added his initials to the "high scores" screen, as number one. Then he turned to Craig.

"Beat that."

"Yeah, kid," added Driscoe.

Craig shrugged his shoulders.

"Ok," he said, stepping up to the machine. "Rob, lend me a quarter."

"Don't ya have any money?"

"Nope."

"What about your allowance?"

"I spent it on comics. Be a pal."

"Alright," Rob relented, fishing a quarter out of his jacket pocket.

Craig inserted his quarter, pressed 'player one' button, gave the controller a slight twist to the right, then pressed fire to begin. The game started, but the board that came up was level five, not the first level.

"Huh?" Tanner exclaim.

Craig spun around the field blasting enemies away. He saved his super-zap for when three red enemies made it to the top. He cleared the level at three thousand two hundred forty points. When he warped past the spikes to the next level, his score jumped up to nineteen thousand two hundred forty points!

"What?" Tanner asked Driscoe.

Driscoe at looked at Tanner slack-jawed, and shrugged.

Craig wasn't done yet. He continued clearing the enemies on the sixth level, using the super-zap once. Although he got hit by the spikes and lost his first man, he proceeded to level seven. That level gave him as hard a time as Tanner had. Craig lost his second life to three red enemies. He managed to clear the field, but lost his final ship to a spike in the warp. His total score was twenty nine thousand one hundred seventy-one. Happily, he put his initials in as high score, bumping Tanner down to second.

"How did you do that?" Tanner demanded.

"It was easy, moron," Craig said with his trademark smile. "If you had read the instructions, or just paid attention to the screen, you would have seen you can use the controller to select a higher level, and extra bonus points, before you start. The higher the level, the more points. So, I started at level five for sixteen thousand bonus points."

"That's cheating!"

"How's it cheating? It's a normal part of the game. So, hand over the cards."

"You think you're so smart, don't you?"

"I'm smarter than you, that's for sure."

Tanner took a couple of threatening steps toward Craig.

"It wasn't fair," Tanner said, giving Craig the dirtiest look he could muster.

"Sounds pretty fair to me," intoned Mr. West, standing just down the aisle from them. "I let all you boys come in here, and play the games for gum, candy and the like. I don't tolerate any cheating, or any poor sports. Give Rick the cards you promised him."

Tanner relented, and tossed the cards at Rick in a huff.

"Come on, Terri."

Tanner and Driscoe left the store, sulking.

"Thanks Mr. West," said Rick.

"Yeah, thanks," added Rob.

"No problem, boys. Just let me know if the older kids are giving you a hard time. I may get busy behind the counter, but remember that you can always count on me."

"We will, Mr. West" said Craig.

11:45am – Goodrich House.

Harriet Goodrich stepped out of her front door, carrying a stepladder in her right arm, and a basket over her left arm. She had spent so much time preparing the candles for the carving contest, she had almost forgotten to put some in her own decorations. She strolled down the front steps, and began to visit each scarecrow one-by-one.

At each scarecrow, she placed the basket down on the ground, planted the stepladder securely, took a single candle out of the basket, and climbed up the ladder. For the scarecrows with pumpkin heads, she simply took the top of the pumpkin off, lit the candle with a lighter, dripped hot wax into the pumpkin, and then placed the extinguished candle inside, using the wax to hold it in place. She then returned the pumpkin top, and climbed down the ladder.

The scarecrows with burlap sacks for heads where a bit more troublesome. After climbing the ladder, she had to lift off the sack over the concealed cast iron lantern underneath. The lantern had to be unlatched in the front, then the candle could be placed inside. After which, she would have to fool with putting the burlap sack back over it. Bothersome, but worth it.

Also, she was using various old iron gardening tools, from rakes, to hoes, to tillers, as the hands on her scarecrows. She wanted to make sure they were all secured to their respective wooden frames. She certainly didn't want to face the embarrassment of one of them falling off. That would never do.

She had to work with expedience though, as she was expecting Billy Weaks to arrive at a quarter to one o'clock. There was much to be done before twilight, when the kids would come out to trick-or-treat, and she didn't want to get behind.

"Time and tide, Mr. Weaks" she said to herself. "Time and tide."

12:01PM – CAROLINA CINEMA.

The boys walked their bikes up the street toward the cinema at Town Square. They hadn't been able to ride, as Rob complained he might spill his drink if they did. When the cinema came into sight, they were greeted by a surprise on the marquee.

"No way."

"How wicked is that?"

Below the large "Carolina Cinema" sign, the multiplex listed both the films for its two auditoriums. In theater one, they were playing *Chariots of Fire*, which the boys only knew as "some movie for old people." In theater two however, they were showing... *Halloween 2*.

"Oh, man. I watched the first one last night on *NBC* with my dad," bragged Rob.

"Yep, me too," said Craig. "I thought it was really cool."

"My favorite part was when she stuck him with the knitting needle."

"I liked it when he was hidden under the bed sheet wearing the glasses."

"I didn't get to watch it," said Rick.

"Why not?"

"My granddad said I'm not old enough."

"Why? It's not really that scary," said Rob.

"Nope, it didn't even have any blood in it," agreed Craig.

"He just said I wasn't old enough."

"Too bad."

The boys continued their walk up the cinema, parked their bikes on the curb, and approached the movie poster display. Craig examined it a moment and then read the tagline aloud:

"*More* of the night *he* came home."

"What? Is it supposed to be the exact same night?" asked Rob.

"Yep."

"Whoa."

Rob considered this for a moment, and then turned to Craig.

"We gotta see it."

"Why?" interrupted Rick.

"How cool would it be to see *Halloween 2*, on Halloween? It's like, I don't know, *double* cool."

"Rob, they won't let us in. It's rated 'R'," said Rick.

"They don't 'let' us in. We sneak in."

"We can't do that!"

"Don't be a sissy. I do it all the time," Rob explained. "We just park our bikes out back around the dumpster. Then we walk inside, and act like we're there to play pinball. We play one game, and when no one is looking, we just go into the theater. They never check inside because they don't want to disturb the people watching the movie."

"I still don't think we should."

"Craig, what do you think?"

"I think your right, Rob. They won't ever find out. Besides, the first one didn't really have anything bad in it."

"I'm afraid we'll get caught."

"You can't be afraid of everything. Rob and I are going to do it. What are you going to do? Just stay out here by yourself the whole time?"

"No."

"Don't worry. It'll be a cinch," said Rob.

"Ok," Rick relented.

"Good. Let's move our bikes around back."

The boys returned to their bikes, and proceeded to walk them around the building's corner to the back, where the dumpster was kept. When they cleared the corner, two figures stood up from behind the parked car, where they had stooped in hiding.

"Aren't you glad we followed them?" asked Driscoe.

"Yep. Easy to do on foot," replied Tanner.

"What do you want to do?"

"We stay here, and watch them go inside. Then we wait. We give them enough time to sneak in. After that, we just walk up to the window, rat them out, and the usher catches them."

"That will show them."

When Craig, Rob and Rick reached the back of the building, they sandwiched their bikes between the dumpster and the wall. Craig then took a large flattened cardboard box he found in the dumpster, and used it to conceal the bikes. Craig turned and addressed Rob.

"You'll have to toss your Big Gulp."

"Why?"

"You know they won't let us bring in our own drinks and stuff. Not even into the lobby," Craig explained.

"Right."

Rob began sucking down his drink very quickly. After only a moment, he could hear the distinct slurping sound of an empty soda cup. He then crushed the cup in his hand, and tossed it triumphantly into the dumpster. The boys then walked back around to the front.

By the time they reached the front of the building, Tanner and Driscoe had returned to their place of hiding. Unaware of the teens' presence the boys walked up to the front door near the box office.

"Remember," whispered Rob "just act natural."

It was Craig that addressed the lady at the window. He glanced at her name badge, casually waved at her, and said:

"Hi Lucy! We're just going in to play *Black Knight*."

Lucy smiled and waved them in. It had become a very common occurrence since the cinema received that game last year. The boys opened the door, and waltzed in toward the machine.

"See, Rick? You just got to be smooth," said Craig.

"I guess so," Rick replied, a bit impressed.

The boys kept their eye on the usher as they moved through the lobby. He was busy taking tickets, and they doubted he even noticed them. They stopped in front of the pinball game, which was located near the entrance to the men's restroom.

"This is a pretty cool game too," commented Craig.

"I know. Two levels, four flippers, and 'Magna-Save!' It even talks,' said Rick.

"Can I get another quarter, Rob?"

"Yeah."

Craig inserted the quarter, causing the choppy synthesized voice to project out of the speakers:

I will slay you, my enemy!

Craig launched the ball into the playing field. He began working the flippers to make as much noise as possible. The machine's verbal taunting also added to boys' cover. He then whispered to Rob:

"Let me know when the usher is busy."

"Will do."

Craig continued to play the pinball game with intense concentration, biding his time. The film had probably already started, so the usher wouldn't be taking tickets much longer. With a little luck, they would only miss the opening credits.

Fight against three enemies!

The game became more fierce, and loud. After a moment Rob leaned over and whispered to him:

"He's walking over to the concession stand!"

Craig glanced over his shoulder.

"Rick, you slip in, and wait for us in the back row."

"Umm…"

"Just go, will ya?!" urged Rob.

Spurred on, Rick turned and quickly walked down the hall to theater two.

Hah-Hah-Hah!

Ha-ha-ha-ha.

"What's he doing now?

"He's helping the girl get more cups out."

"Ok, you go."

Rob hesitated.

"You sure?"

"Yep!"

Rob walked very fast, and very stiffly into the theater. Craig continued playing the game, glancing back and forth from the game to the concession stand.

Hah-Hah-Hah!

Ha-ha-ha-ha.

After another moment, the usher reached down under the counter to retrieve something. Craig took his hands off the flippers, and calmly strolled down the hall, unseen.

One enemy cannot fight the Black Knight again!

12:35pm – Theater 2.

Craig entered the half empty theater, and found the other two boys waiting for him in the back row. He preferred sitting as close as possible to the screen, but here in the back, no one was likely to notice that they were in the theater alone. He took the seat next to Rob, and stared up at the screen. On it, a jack-o-lantern flickered in the darkness. The film's distinctive theme filled the auditorium.

"Did I miss anything?"

"No," answered Rob. "They pretty much just re-showed the ending of the first one, then the opening credits started to roll."

"Awesome," he replied. He then looked over his shoulder back at the door. "Hey, let's slide down all the way to the other side."

"Why?"

"That way, if someone comes in through the door, they won't see us."

"Good idea," said Rick, who quickly made is way down to the far end of the back row. His friends just behind him. They all then took their seats in confidence.

Rob leaned over and whispered to Rick.

"See? No problem at all."

Tanner and Driscoe waited to about 12:40pm before approaching the lady at the ticket window. Before speaking, Tanner peered inside the lobby through the glass door, and saw that no one was standing near the pinball game. Tanner then summoned his best 'Eddie Haskell' impression.

"Excuse me, Miss… Lucy?"

"Yes?"

"Did you see three kids come in here a short while ago?"

"Yes, they went in to play pinball. Are you looking for one of them?"

"No ma'am." Tanner paused, briefly. "Gosh, I don't want to cause any trouble. But my friend and I were down at the 7-Eleven earlier, and we overheard those kids talking about sneaking in to see the new *Halloween* movie."

Lucy looked back, over at the pinball machine, and saw the kids were not at it. Tanner continued:

"I almost didn't want to say anything, but I figured it was the right thing to do. They shouldn't be in an 'R' rated film by themselves. It could get the theater owner in trouble."

Lucy craned her neck around, trying to spot the usher. When she saw him helping out at the concession stand, she turned back to Tanner.

"Can you do me a favor?" she asked. "Can you go tell what you told me to that man over at the concession stand?" She pointed the usher out to Tanner.

"Yes ma'am, I can."

Driscoe had to look down at his shoes, and bite his lip to keep from smiling.

The boys were engrossed in watching the film. Rick had already slouched down in his chair for some sense of protection from the foreboding events he was seeing on screen. Rob had started to sweat and squirm quite a bit, but he nervously blamed that on the stuffiness of the room. Even Craig wasn't very cavalier anymore. He had discovered that there was a big

46

difference between watching a horror movie in the comfort of his own lighted living room, and watching one in the darkness of a lonely theater.

"You ok, Rob?" gulped Craig.

"Yeah, you?" Rob said, his eyes locked on the screen, like a deer frozen in headlights.

"Fine. Rick?"

Rick remained in stunned silence.

"Rick?"

"Rick, you gonna be ok?" asked Rob.

Rick finally replied:

"Not for a very long time."

It was then that the boys heard the theater door open, and saw a man with a flashlight come through it. Craig looked over to his friends in wide-eyed horror.

"Into the aisle!" he order in a hushed voice. The boys piled into the opposite aisle and tried to conceal themselves. As they did, the movie's frightening score kicked in. The usher ominously began shining his light around, looking for something.

"Is he looking for us?" asked Rob.

"Yep," replied Craig.

"How did he find out?"

Just then, Tanner and Driscoe entered the theater, and began craning their necks to look around.

"Those *barf bags*," said Rob.

"Listen, we just crawl down the aisle until we get to the bottom," Craig said, pointing where to go. "Then we run through the fire exit, and get on our bikes."

"I told you we shouldn't have done this."

"Just go."

Craig took point as the boys began to crawl feverishly down the aisle on their hands and knees, their speed being driven by the rising tempo of the score. Each one hoped they wouldn't be seen under the cover of darkness.

The usher began shining his light up and down each row as he made his way through the rows, one-by-one. The other patrons began to grumble, waving away the bright light, and looking around, wondering what the commotion was about. Some stood up from their seats. The music continued to fill the air.

Trying to get a better vantage point, Tanner hopped up onto one of the unoccupied seats, stood with one foot on each of the armrests, and surveyed the whole theater. He tried to see by the light reflected off the screen itself, but the scene showing was at night, and provided no luminance.

Then, as luck would have it, at around eighteen minutes and twenty seconds into the film, Tanner heard the roar of a screeching car blare over the speakers, followed by the rumble of an explosion, as a fiery blast on the screen lit up the whole theater! He spied what he was looking for.

"They're crawling down the aisle towards the fire door!" he shouted.

Craig jumped to his feet.

"Run!"

The boys ran like crazy toward the door. The usher ran down the aisle, and crossed in front of the screen after them.

48

Craig pushed open the fire door with a shove!

Rob grabbed their makeshift cardboard wall and tossed it aside!

Rick ran behind the dumpster, hopped on his bike and rode off as fast as his legs could pedal him.

Quickly, the other two boys did the same, first Craig, then Rob.

The usher, followed by Tanner and Driscoe, came running out of the theater after them. They all tried catch the boys, but the usher quickly became winded, and had to relent. Tanner and Driscoe fared better, following the trio as they turned east on Harvest Rd, riding away from Town Square. After a couple of minutes, they too gave up the chase, conceding to the boys' head start.

"I'm gonna get them yet," spat Tanner. Furiously, he made his way back toward the Town Square. As he drew closer, he noticed Mr. Porter, Mr. Tallman and Mrs. Sutter walking from the pavilion, across the street, towards *Morty's Country Diner*.

Tanner smiled at Driscoe.

"Follow me."

12:45pm – Goodrich House.

Billy Weaks rode a 1980 Huffy Pro Thunder. The *Thunder* had a silver frame with blue lettering. It had a blue hand brake, blue handlebars, blue padding, blue nameplate, *amazing* blue Lester Mag wheels, and even blue rubber tires, albeit dirty ones. Although a Christmas gift from his folks, Billy give little thought to its upkeep, relying on his dad to keep the chain oiled, and tires inflated. It's not that he didn't like the bike, he did. It rode well. It's just that he couldn't be bothered with all of that. There was *Atari 2600* to be played.

Billy rode up Old Mill Rd. to Miss Goodrich's home. The house was an old large wooden home that sat on a piece of land at the corner of Old Mill and Spring Ave. It appeared to have two stories, and an attic. He would guess there was a basement also. He marveled at all the Halloween scarecrows that decorated the yard. Neat! He rode his bike up to her front yard, then up the center path, between her two old trees, right to the porch. There he found Harriet Goodrich waiting for him. She was seated in an old rocking chair, sipping a cup of what he assumed was steaming tea.

"Mr. Weaks, I admit to being a little bit surprised. You are on time."

"My dad said I had to be," he huffed. "He says I gotta habit of being late everywhere, and I gotta stop."

"Your father is a wise man. Timing is everything. As you get older, you become more aware of how precious time really is."

"If you say so."

Harriet stood up, and smiled at the boy. The wind caught her grey/white hair, causing it dance around the sides of her face.

"I do say so Mr. Weaks. I do."

Billy was silent for a moment.

"What all did you need me to do?"

"Nothing fancy. I just need you to rake up all of the leaves on the ground. Collect them up, then dump them in my compost heap in the back, next to the cellar door. When you're done, come see me in the kitchen."

"Ok."

"The rake is at the side of the house, next to the wheel barrel."

Billy just nodded.

"I'll be inside."

Harriet returned to inside her home, leaving Billy alone. He sighed, and walked around the side of the house to find the tools she had mentioned. He placed the head of the rake in the wheel barrel, with its handle resting on his shoulder. He then grabbed the two handles of the wheel barrel, and rolled them both into the front yard. He decided to start at the very edge of the yard first, and work his way to the back. When he reached the edge, he sighed, took hold of the rake, and began to clean up the leaves, muttering to himself.

"I've gotta start getting to school on time."

1:20pm – Old Mill Rd.

After a half hour of solid pedaling, the boys felt sure that they were in the clear, and began to slow down. They hadn't risked continuing up Main St, so they cut across Harvest Rd, and then followed Old Mill Rd to the north. The road ran parallel to Main St, and had actually once been the town's central boulevard. Therefore, the houses on the road where older than most others in town, and thus home to older residents. This made the whole neighborhood prime pickings for kids on Halloween, as everyone knew that the elderly bought the best candy.

"I'm going to be in so much trouble."

"Rick, don't worry about it. Your grandad will never even find out about it."

"He's right," agreed Rob. "That doofus usher never got a good look at us. Besides, he don't know who we are, so there's *no way* he can call our parents."

"Maybe. I just wish I hadn't snuck in. That's all."

"Just chill Rick," said Craig.

"Yeah, we can always back each other up with our folks," added Rob.

Craig suddenly slammed on his brakes, and stopped his bike.

"Doesn't old lady Goodrich live up this way?"

"I don't know," said Rick.

"Yeah, she does," answered Rob. "My brother used to mow her lawn in the summer."

"I've got an idea!"

"What?"

"This morning, Billy Weaks said he was going over there to help rake up her yard and stuff."

"So?"

"So? We ride up there, and offer to help him rake up, or anything else he needs. In exchange, we get him to say we were helping him the whole time. That way, if our folks ask, we couldn't have possibly been at the theater."

"I don't think that's a good idea."

"No, I think it's a *great* idea," said Rob. "Better safe than sorry."

"Rick, this way we're covered, no matter what."

Rick looked down at the road for a moment, in thought.

"Ok, but no more sneaking into anything."

"We promise."

The boys continued on their bikes up Mill Rd for a few more minutes. In the distance, they caught sight of Billy Weaks pushing a wheel barrel around the side of the house. The three then started to head directly to him, toward Miss Goodrich's back yard.

Billy had been raking for a while now, and had decided to start carrying some of the leaves around back. He was worried that strong winds would undo his efforts. He had loaded up the wheel barrel with several armfuls, and headed around the house to dump them in the compost heap.

He rounded the corner of the house and saw the cellar door Miss Goodrich had mentioned. It was the traditional "storm cellar" type, whose frame connected to the house at about a forty-five degree angle. Attached to the frame were two heavy double doors. This was a very common feature for homes in the area. Billy didn't immediately see the compost heap, so he figured it was located on the opposite side of the frame.

When he arrived on the other side of the cellar doors, he found the ground there to be devoid of compost also. He looked at the ground quizzically, parked the wheel barrel, and walked back to the other side again. Still, no trace it was used for compost. In fact, the ground on *both* sides of the cellar frame looked pretty clean.

Maybe she meant I was supposed to start a brand new heap on either side? Maybe I should just pick a side? No, if I do, she'll just say she wanted it on the other side instead. Grownups are like that. They don't care if they're right or wrong. It's their way, because they say so.

As Billy stood in thought, the cellar door began to shake slightly.

Thump-thump

Thump-thump.

The noise caught Billy's attention. He stood in front of the door to see if the latch was loose or something, but it stopped shaking just as suddenly as it started.

"Huh?"

Billy started to walk away, but the doors began to quake again.

Thump-thump

Thump-thump.

*Thump-thump-**thump!***

Then silence again.

"What the?"

Thump-Thump-Thump-Thump.

*Thump-**Thump!-Thump!***

THump-THump-THump-THump.

THump-THump!-THump!

Silence.

In the back of Billy's mind, he knew he wanted to move, to get away, but he felt as if his body was frozen in place. The doors started up once more.

Thump-Thump.

***Thump!**-Thump!-Thump!*

THump-THump.

*THump!-THump!-**THump!***

THUmp-THUmp-THUmp-THUump.

*THUmp!-**THUmp!**-THUmp!*

THUMp-THUMp-THUMp-THUMp.

*THUMp!-THUMp!-**THUMp!***

THUMP-THUMP-THUMP-THUMP.

THUMP!-THUMP!-THUMP!

Violently, the doors swung open, as a tremendous gust of wind blew out from inside the cellar itself.

Craig, Rob and Rick were coasting their bikes around the side of the house, when the three started to hear a loud ruckus coming from the back. They just rounded the corner when they saw the cellar doors blow open, while Billy stood static in front of them. A huge gust of howling wind followed the doors. It blew leaves and dirt everywhere. The linens on the laundry lines flapped in the wind. A few drying pillow cases blew away. The boys had to shield their eyes with their hands to see through the dust that was kicked up. The noise was deafening.

"What's happening?!" exclaimed Rick.

Then, the boys saw a sight that boggled their collective minds.

In almost an instant, dozens of wispy thin black tentacles shot out of the cellar, like dark bolts of sinister lightning striking suddenly out of a stormy night sky. They wrapped Billy up in their cold choking embrace, and yanked him down into the cellar. The doors flew closed behind them with a thud, and outside everything became eerily calm again.

"I told you this wasn't a good idea."

1:29pm – Goodrich House.

"What was that?!"

"Quiet Rob, it'll know we're here."

"We've got to get Billy out of there," said Rick running up to the door.

Craig gave chase. Rob followed.

"Wait. Wait. Wait," Craig called to him in hushed tones.

Rick reached the doors, and was about to start pounding on them with his fist, when Craig grabbed ahold of his arm.

"Rick, don't."

"But we've got to get him out of there."

"We can't do anything for him, if those things pull us down there with him."

"Right."

"What're we gonna do?" asked Rob.

"Is there cellar window?"

The boys immediately began scanning the back of the building.

"Not back here, at least."

"There might be a window on one of the sides," said Rick. "Did we pass one coming back here?"

"I didn't see one."

"There should be one, for extra light. Maybe there is one on the other side?"

"Good thinking, Rick! Come on, Rob."

The boys ran to the opposite side of the house that they had passed by just moments ago. Just around the corner, they saw a small cellar window at ground level. Craig and Rick flanked each side of the window.

"What am I supposed to do?" asked Rob.

"Be our lookout," replied Craig.

Rob began looking around in all directions, keeping his eye out for anything.

"Can you see anything, Rick?"

"No, the window's too dirty."

"Can you hear anything?"

"No."

Craig felt around the top of the window, then the bottom. It appeared to be hinged at the top, and to open outward. He dug his fingers around the bottom crack, and forced some of them in. He then slowly pulled the window open, upward and outward. It only opened perhaps an inch or two, but it was enough to look in the cellar via the window's sides. Both he and Rick had to lie on their stomachs to peer in.

It was hard to see much in the cellar, as it was dark, save for the light shining down the stairs from the open kitchen door. In the middle of the room was a large cobblestone well, flanked on each side by what appeared to be unlit torches. Various pieces of old furniture, dusty crates, and the like, filled some of the space against the walls. Billy Weaks was lying on his side on the floor, hogtied with a towel stuffed in his mouth. Harriet Goodrich was kneeling behind him, tying the knot.

Craig looked over his shoulder, and whispered to Rob.

"Rob, you have got to see this."

Rob ran over to Craig, and lied next to him, looking over his shoulder. It wasn't the best view, but it would do.

Inside, Harriet had just finished her knot. She then patted Billy on the head and smiled.

"There Mr. Weaks, you are now tightly secured," she said in her typically sweet style.

Billy tried to yell at her through the muffling towel, but it was to no avail.

"Helmph! Helllmph! Hellllmph!"

"Go ahead, yell all you want to young man," she said. "All it will do is get you winded. If you're tired out, it will only make my task later all that easier."

"Whumph arf ooo doofeem oof cwaffy laalee?!"

"What am I doing? Why Mr. Weaks, I am doing whatever pleases me."

"Helmph! Helllmph! Hellllmph!"

Harriet leaned in closer, and whispered in his ear.

"If you really must know. This evening, I'm going to come back down here, pick you up, and throw you down that well."

"Helmph! Helllmph! Hellllmph!"

"Helmph! Helllmph! Hellllmph!"

Harriet stood up, flung her head back, and let out a loud metallic sounding cackle. As she did, her eyes lit-up red like fire.

"Eeeeh-hee-hee-hee-hee-heeee!"

Outside the window, Craig and Rob looked at each other, and gasped. Inside, a terrified Billy tried to scream louder, as Harriet stood over him, her body now contorted in a twisted manner.

"HELmph! HELLLmph! HELLLLmph!"

"No one can save you! Nothing can stop my plan, set in motion long ago," she said in an echoing metallic voice, her eyes glowing even brighter. "Decades past, we witches were banished from our home world. We were forced, by scientific ritual, down through the celestial causeways, and across the great sullen void. We became exiles from our own galaxy. In a weakened state, we were left to perish on this backwater piece of filth you call Earth. Now, after years of grueling research, of meticulous calculations, and of unwavering patience, I have completed the portal I need."

Harriet motioned to the well.

"I dug the pit myself, and built the walls with my own hands. It wasn't easy. There were exact measurements to follow. It had to be ten feet wide, and three hundred fifty-three feet deep, no more, no less. The walls had to be made from Preseli Spotted Dolerite, taken from the hills of Wales. It took years to slowly import all the rock that I needed. I had to do it one stone at a time.

Finally, it is complete! The portal is ready, but I need the power of 'Light Magic' to break the barricade between our worlds. That is where you come in. All mortal beings in the universe are gifted with a special magic at birth, the 'Child Magic'. It is one of the most powerful forms of Light Magic in existence, but you mortals foolishly waste it, and let it fade away as you age. Yours will not go to waste though. I have good use for it.

Tonight, on *Hallow'eve*, when the sun sets, and twilight comes upon us, the Child Magic within you will be at its strongest! When it is, I will hurl you down the well! It will cause an explosion that will crack open the barrier to my world. Then, my coven, awaiting me on the other side, will fly through it to this world. United once more, our powers will be complete, and we will reign terror upon your world, and all others, the likes of which no mortal eye has ever seen!"

Harriet cackled louder and more gleefully than even before.

"Eeeeh-hee-hee-hee-hee-heeee!"

"HELmph! HELLLmph! HELLLLmph!"

"Eeeeh-hee-hee-hee-hee-heeee!"

Harriet suddenly snapped back into her kindly façade. She pressed her hands together, as if in prayer, and smiled the sweetest smile in the world.

"Now, you'll have to excuse me Mr. Weaks. I have so much to do before tonight."

Harriet turned and made her way up the stairs. When she reached the door, she stopped and turned back to face Billy.

"I think the whole town will find this Halloween, a very memorable one."

Harriet then strode through the doorway, and slammed it shut behind her, leaving Billy alone in the dark.

"HELmph! HELLLmph! HELLLLmph!"

Outside, the shocked boys rolled up from their prone positions, into seated ones, backs against the wall. Craig shook his head in disbelief.

"I don't believe it. Miss Goodrich…is a… a… witch."

"Not just a *witch*, but an evil *space-witch*," add Rick.

"But she makes such good cookies," said Rob.

"We've got to help Billy," said Rick.

"I ain't goin' in there with no witch."

"But Rob, we have to!"

"Rob is right. We can't go in there. Whatever it was that grabbed Billy might still be around. What we have to do is go get help."

"That makes sense."

Rick got back down on his stomach and pressed his face up against the window opening. In a hushed voice he called inside:

"Billy! Billy!"

Billy heard Rick's voice and looked over to the window.

"HELmph! HELLLmph! HELLLLmph!"

"Billy! It's me. It's Rick Davenport!"

"HELmph!"

"You hold on. I'm here with Craig and Rob. We're going to go get help. Ok?"

Billy nodded vigorously.

Rick hopped to his feet. The others joined him. Craig laid out the plan.

"First, we go grab our bikes. Then we ride down the street a few houses, and knock on a door for help. We call the sheriff, and wait for him."

"Let's go!"

1:41pm – Old Mill Rd.

The boys rode down the street, picked a house at random, rode their bikes right up the walkway to the porch. They dropped their bikes on the lawn and ran up the steps. Rob frantically knocked on the door several times. He waited a moment, and when no one answered he knocked several times more. This time, the door opened and an elderly man, answered them.

"You boys need to stop knocking on my door! I don't care for trick-or-treaters!"

"We're not here for trick-or-treating," stated Rick frankly.

"I don't care what you are, or aren't here for, you just need to go away!"

"We just need to use your phone," said Craig.

"Well, you can't use it."

"Why not?"

"It's my home, I don't have to explain anything to you *hooligans*."

"Please, we need to call the sheriff," he explained.

"The sheriff?"

"Yes!"

"What for?"

"Look mister, we're all in trouble. It turns out that old lady Goodrich is a space-witch, and she has friend of ours locked-up in her cellar!" Rob blurted out in frustration.

"No, *you* look! I don't care for kids, and I certainly don't care for their shenanigans! If you think I'm going to let you use my phone to prank call the sheriff, you have another thing coming!"

"Please, we're *serious*," pleaded Rick.

"You're in *serious trouble* you mean! I think you're the same lot that egged my house last year."

"But we didn't!"

The man pointed his finger right at Rob.

"I remember you! I saw you riding away on that yellow bike of yours! It *was* you!"

"No, that wasn't me! It was probably my brother Paul. This used to be his bike!"

"Hah! *Liar!* Now, you kids get off my lawn, take your bikes with you, and just go away! You better leave my house alone, and not come back here, or I'll be the one calling the sheriff on *you*."

"But you've got to help us!"

"I don't *got* to do anything. I certainly don't *got* to take orders from a bunch of delinquents. Now go!

The man then slammed the door shut. The boys could hear the deadbolt being locked on the other side.

"Let's try the next house," Craig said.

The boys ran across the lawn to the neighboring home. They climbed up the steps to the porch, and Craig rang the doorbell. He waited patiently a moment, and rang it again.

"There's no car in the driveway. Maybe no one is home," suggested Rick.

"Maybe. I'll just ring it one more time."

Craig did so, and the boys waited a couple minutes more.

"Let's just go on to the next one," said Rob.

The boys ran down the porch steps, then heard the old man next door call out to them.

"I told you boys to get your bikes off my lawn! You didn't do that! Now, I've called the sheriff and they're sending someone over in a car to pick you hoodlums up!"

"But we didn't do anything!" exclaimed Rick.

"We're trying to help!" shouted Craig.

"The only thing you're doing is being a pain! I said get your stinking bikes off my lawn! I'm going to go get my bat and bust them all up!"

The man went back into his house to retrieve his baseball bat. Craig, Rick and Rob ran back into his yard, hopped on their bikes, and rode off.

"Why don't we just wait until the police car arrives? Then, we can tell them everything." suggested Rick.

"They wouldn't believe us. We're kids, he's an old man, he can make up any story he likes, and the cops will just believe him no matter what," explained Craig.

"What're we gonna do?" asked Rob.

"Let's ride back to the store, and see if Mr. West will listen to us."

The boys pedaled their bikes with all the strength and speed they could muster. There was no time to be tired, far too much depended on them getting help in time.

2:22PM – Town Square.

The boys raced down Old Mill Rd, turned right onto Harvest, and pulled into Town Square. They hooked a left, and rode straight up to the 7-Eleven. Leaving their bikes by the ice freezer, they quickly made their way into the store.

"Mr. West! Mr. West!" called Rick.

Behind the counter was a young man named Pat Rosen. He spoke to the boys as he wiped down the counter.

"Mr. West is off for the rest of the day," said Pat. "He had to leave a little early to go trick-or-treating with his grandkids in Charleston."

Rob sighed deeply. Rick slapped his hands against the side of his head.

"Of course he did," said Craig in defeat.

"Can I help you boys with something?" Pat asked.

"No, you wouldn't believe us" said Rob.

"C'mon guys, let's go," said Craig, leading the others back outside.

"What are we going to do now?" asked Rick.

"I don't know."

"We gotta do something!" said Rob.

"We should call my grandad," suggested Rick. "We'll ask him to drive down here, and take us over to Miss Goodrich's house. Then, we can take him around back, and show him Billy through the window."

"Do you think he'll do it?"

Rick shook his head.

"I don't know."

A voice called from across the street.

"Hey boys! You there. You kids!"

The boys looked over in the direction of the voice, and saw Sheriff Josh Wilson walking towards them. They froze like three deer caught in headlights.

"Were you three over at the cinema earlier?" Sheriff Wilson demanded.

"Well, we... we..: stammered Craig.

"That's them Sheriff!" said a familiar voice, calling from across the road. "Those are the kids we saw. We saw them do it."

It was Tanner Blake. He began to cross the street after the sheriff.

"Oh man," said Rob.

Sheriff Wilson walked up to the boys, notepad in hand, and began to question them.

"I understand you three were caught sneaking into an 'R' rated film earlier today. What do you have to say for yourselves?"

"Look, we shouldn't have done that! It was stupid! I didn't want to, but I let them talk me into it. It's my fault!" exclaimed Rick.

"Rick!" interrupted Craig.

"Uh-huh," said the sheriff. "I also got a report from Hoyt Williams that you boys were running around his whole neighborhood, ringing everyone's doorbells, and running off."

"That's not true. We didn't do that," said Craig. "Look, we rang his doorbell, but it's because we needed to use his phone."

"I understand you wanted to use it to crank call me."

"That's not true, he made that up!"

"He also said that one of you egged his house."

"That wasn't me, it was my brother!" cried Rob.

"Uh-huh. Your brother was with you today?"

"Not today, he means *last* Halloween!"

"Uh-huh. You boys are in a lot of trouble. Pulling pranks and stupid stunts is one thing, but destroying someone's property is another."

"What?" Craig asked.

"Now, tell me the truth. Which one of you vandalized Jake Tallman's pick-up truck?"

"What??" Craig repeated.

"It was that one," said Tanner, pointing. "Craig Chambers. I saw him do it."

"What?"

"After they ran out of the movie, they rode back around and spray painted Mr. Tallman's truck. They did it while he was at lunch with Mr. Porter and Mrs. Sutter. I saw him do it, and tried to catch them, but they're too fast on their bikes. So, I ran over to the diner to tell Mr. Tallman."

"We didn't do that!" pleaded Rick.

"You watch your tone of voice with me, son!" snapped the sheriff.

"But we didn't!"

"You mean to tell me you didn't do that?" the sheriff said, pointing to Jake Tallman's truck. Written on the side of it, in bright orange spray paint were the words:

'HaPpy HaLLoWeen'

"No, we didn't!"

"I want you three to follow me over to my car, and I'll have dispatch call your parents."

"But we didn't do that!!" pleaded Rick, again.

"I said, watch your tone of voice with me!" the sheriff ordered. "Now, follow me."

The Sheriff walked them over to his car, and took their names, addresses and phone numbers. He then radioed into the station to have their parents contacted, and told to come pick up their children at the Town Square pavilion. Busy with his work, he failed to see Tanner and Driscoe giving each other a 'high five' across the street.

3:53pm – 1717 Fleet St.

"Jeff, this is your fault!" blasted Amanda Hanson.

"How is this my fault?" he asked.

"You let him watch those scary movies, and read those scary books. They give him ideas."

"Nothing in those things tell him to vandalize cars."

"They tell him it's ok to scare people, and that inspires him to pull pranks and cause trouble."

"What trouble has he caused up to this point?"

"You don't think that this is enough? What do you want him to do? Slash people's tires and burn things down?"

"You're blowing this way out of proportion."

"He spray-painted graffiti on Jake Tallman's truck!"

"They said the Chambers' boy did that."

"That still makes Rob an accessory."

"Doesn't anyone want to hear what I have to say?" begged Rob.

"No!" Rob's parents answered in unison.

"Go upstairs to your room, and stay there until you're told to come down!" she ordered.

"But mom, I told you, I didn't do it!"

"Go upstairs!" she repeated.

Rob shrugged and made his way slowly up the steps. He took a left at the top, and trudged his way into his room, closing the door behind him. Rob sat on the bed with a thump. He could still hear the sound of his parents arguing with each other downstairs.

3:56PM – 1713 FLEET ST.

"How could you embarrass us like this, Craig?" asked Carlton Chambers.

"I'm on the PTA, for goodness' sake," added his mother, Debbie.

"I didn't mean to."

"You didn't mean to sneak into the movies? You didn't mean to run around knocking on everyone's doors? You didn't mean to paint 'Happy Halloween' on Jake Tallman's Chevy?"

"I meant, I didn't mean to embarrass you."

"What did you think was going to happen?"

"Do you know what people are going to say? We're going to be the talk of the whole town for a month."

"Not true, there won't be a town in a month," said Craig.

"We should be so lucky."

"No, not really," Craig replied, shaking his head.

"I'm tired of your smart talk, Craig."

"It's not smart talk, it's the truth."

"Craig, when you say things like that, people are going to wonder where you got the ideas from. It makes the whole family look foolish."

"You two are always worried about what everyone else 'thinks'. Well, no one in town is going to be 'thinking' *anything* after tonight, so you don't have to worry about it." Craig said, making his way to the stairs. "Granted, that's because there won't *be* a town for them to 'think' *in*, but who cares as long as you're not embarrassed, right?" He then started to ascend the steps.

"Where do you think you're going, young man?"

"My room. That's where you going to send me, right?"

His parents remained silent.

"Well, ok then," he said. Craig then walked upstairs to his room, and closed the door behind him.

3:58pm – 1714 Fleet St.

"I'm sorry Rick. I feel that I've failed you," said Mathew Davenport.

"You haven't, grandpa."

"Rick, I've tried to raise you the best I can. It hasn't always been easy, but I thought I had at least taught you right from wrong."

"You did," said Rick sheepishly.

"Then explain your behavior to me."

"It started when we were at the 7-Eleven. We were playing a video game. Tanner Blake and his friend Driscoe were giving us a hard time. Craig beat them at a game, and called them some names, so they got mad at us. Mr. West had to run them off. He'd tell you that if he wasn't in Charleston. Then, we walked down to the theater to play pinball."

Rick took a breath and continued.

"When Craig and Rob saw what movie was playing, they wanted to sneak inside. I didn't want to, but they said they were going to do it anyway, even if they went in without me. I should have still said no, but I didn't want to be left by myself. After we snuck in, the usher came in looking for us. Tanner and Driscoe were with him, so they must have been following us. We ran out, and rode up Old Mill Rd. That's when we saw Billy Weaks get taken."

"You saw him get *taken*?"

"Yes, these thin tentacles came out of Miss Goodrich's cellar and grabbed him. That's the truth."

"I see. When did Craig spray paint Mr. Tallman's truck?"

"He didn't! Tanner and Driscoe just made that up."

"Why were you boys running up and down the street ringing people's doorbells and running away?"

"We didn't. Mr. Williams made that up too. When we saw what happened to Billy we wanted to get help. We knocked on his door for help, that's all. When he wouldn't listen to us, we tried next door, but they weren't at home. Then, he said he'd call the sheriff on us."

"Why would Mr. Williams make something like that up?"

"I don't know. Maybe he didn't mean to lie. Maybe he just imagined it wrong in his mind."

"Could it be what you said about Billy Weaks, about tentacles grabbing him, could it be that you imagined that wrong in your mind as well?"

"No. It's what really happened."

"Rick, things like that don't really happen. Monsters, and witches, and all the like, they don't exist."

"I know, but maybe *she* exists because she's from another planet. Maybe they do have witches on other planets."

"Rick, they don't have witches on other planets either."

"How do you know? Have you ever been to one?"

"Rick, go up to your room, and let me think about all of this. I need to figure out what I've done wrong in raising you. Then, we'll work on setting things right, together."

"Yes sir," said Rick, starting up the stairs. He turned back to his grandad solemnly. "Grandpa Matt, what if I'm right? What if Billy is down there and needs help?"

"Rick…"

"Maybe I did imagine it wrong in my mind. Maybe he just fell down the cellar door. Maybe Miss Harriet isn't a witch. But, what if Billy does need help. Would you want *me* left there by myself?"

"No Rick, of course not. Now, go on up to your room. We'll talk about this later."

Reluctantly, Rick followed his grandad's orders, and confined himself to his room.

Matthew Davenport sat alone in thought for a moment. He then looked over at the telephone hanging on the wall, and stared at it intently.

4:03PM – TOWN SQUARE

Margie pressed her finger against the bright green pumpkin she had painted. It wasn't even tacky. She checked a few of the other ones, and they had already dried.

"These look good, Edgar. Let's pick them up, and make a few piles of them next to the pavilion."

Edgar joined her in stacking the dayglow pumpkins neatly on the right hand side of the center pavilion. The larger pumpkins had to go on bottom to keep the piles from falling over. The few with uneven bottoms would have to be placed on the ground separately. Margie took extra care in making sure the various colors were spread out evenly in the piles.

Jake Tallman exited the square's phone booth and jogged back over to the pavilion. He rejoined Margie and Edgar, and helped them with the pumpkin piles.

"What did old Gus say, Jake?"

"He said that it's unlikely the spray paint will come off. He's gonna try a couple of things, but he said that he'd give me a special deal on having it sanded down and repainted."

"I imagine that Mr. Davenport, the Hansons, and the Chambers would pay for it."

"I'm sure they will, Ed. But that doesn't mean I can't still get a good deal on it."

"You're a saint Jake," said Margie.

"I do what I can."

When they finished stacking the pumpkins, Margie stepped back and examined them

"They look beautiful, Jake."

"Thank you."

"I almost forgot our sign!" said Edgar, rushing over to where he had been working. He picked up a wooden sign, attached to a stake, and planted it next to the pumpkins. In bright fluorescent colors it said: The Magic Pumpkin Patch.

"I cut a stencil out of a piece of poster board, then just sprayed it with the leftover paint," he explained.

"That's good thinking, Ed."

"It's a wonderful sign, Ed," added Margie. "Jake, you start setting up the folding tables, and I'll finish up the booths. Ed, I need you to run across the street and pick up the cotton candy machine from *Morty's*. With everything else going on, I almost forgot about it."

"Will do! Be back in jiff."

Ed waved at her and trotted across the street to the diner. As he did, a mother walking with her young child passed by him, making her way to the pavilion.

"Afternoon, Lydia!" he said.

"Afternoon, Mr. Porter!"

With her daughter in hand, Lydia Small approached Margie.

"Hello, Mrs. Sutter!"

"Why Lydia Small, how are you young lady?

"Just fine ma'am."

"Is this little Megan? She has grown like a weed."

"Say hello to Mrs. Sutter, Megan."

"Hello."

"My goodness. You are making me feel old. Miss Megan, did you know I used to be your momma's teacher?"

"No."

"No *what*, Megan?"

"No, ma'am."

Margie smiled. It was nice to see a parent raising her child with manners.

"So, are you two coming to the Festival tonight?"

"No, ma'am. I want to go trick-or-treating."

"Oh Megan, we can still find time to stop by tonight."

"But I don't want to miss trick-or-treating."

"You'll have to forgive her, Mrs. Sutter. She's got her heart set on it."

"Oh, I understand. Children that young might get bored at the festival with all of us 'old folks'." Margie laughed. "Besides, there's always next year. Right?"

Megan nodded.

"Mommy, can we go pick up my bunny costume?"

"Yes sweetie. We had to have Pete Rucker order her costume, because he ran out of bunny ones."

"I see. Well, you have fun trick-or-treating tonight Megan."

"I will."

"Goodbye, Mrs. Sutter. Say goodbye to Mrs. Sutter, Megan."

"Goodbye, Mrs. Sutter."

"Goodbye, young lady."

Lydia took Megan by the hand, and they made their way across the street to *Rucker's* store.

"Cute as a button!" said Jake.

"Yes, she's a little darling."

"I wasn't talking about her."

"Oh Jake Tallman, you quit!"

4:04pm – 1714 Fleet St.

"Hello? Mrs. Weaks?"

"Yes."

"This is Matt Davenport. My grandson Rick knows your boy, Billy."

"Oh, I think I know Rick. Sweet little boy, right?"

"Yes. Yes, he is… Um, Rick was telling me that your boy was doing some yard work for Harriet Goodrich today?"

"He is, why?"

"Oh, I'm just trying to confirm something that Rick told me. It seems Rick and some of his friends got into a bit of trouble earlier today, but he says they were visiting with Billy there, when the worst of the *alleged* shenanigans were supposed to be happening."

"Oh?"

"Yes. So, I was wondering, about what time was young Billy was over at Miss Goodrich's?"

"Well, he was supposed to be at her house at about a quarter until one."

"As far as you know, did he arrive promptly?"

"I believe he did. If he didn't, I'm sure Harriet would have called us up, and had a fit about it."

"I see. What time did Billy make it back home?"

"He didn't."

"Ma'am?"

"Billy decided to spend Halloween night over at one of his friend's house. Miss Goodrich called and told us she had given him a lift down there."

"I'd like to talk to Billy, and see if he can confirm Rick's side of the story. Who is he staying with?"

"Chris King, they have sleepovers all the time."

"Chris? Is that Jolene and Archie King's boy?"

"Yes, it is."

"Would you mind if I called and asked Billy about this afternoon?"

"I don't see why not, as long as you don't spoil his sleepover."

"Oh, no ma'am. I just want to know if he saw Rick today or not."

"That should be fine then."

"Thank you for your time, Mrs. Weaks."

"You're very welcome, Mr. Davenport."

Matthew Davenport hung up the phone. He then began to thumb through the phone book. He located the number for Archie Weaks, and dialed it on his rotary phone.

Ring-ring.

I'm sure this whole thing is just a misunderstanding.

Ring-ring.

Rick would never go around ringing people's doorbells and then run off.

Ring-ring.

I taught Rick better than that.

Ring-ring.

I know my boy.

Ring-ring.

He's a good boy.

Ring-ring.

I bet it really was Tanner Blake that did that to Jake Tallman's car.

Ring-ring.

Why aren't these folks answering?

Ring-ring.

They could be out.

Ring-ring.

But it's too early for trick-or-treating.

Ring-ring.

What if Billy really did fall?

Ring-ring.

But Mrs. Weaks said Miss Goodrich drove him to the King's home.

Ring-ring.

So, he must be alright.

Ring-ring.

Right?

Ring-ring.

I mean, why would Miss Goodrich lie?

Ring-ring.

Mr. Davenport hung up the phone. After a second's worth of thought, he picked it up again, and dialed a different number.

"Hello?"

"Judy? It's Matt Davenport from across the street."

"Hello, Mr. Davenport."

"Is Tina at home right now?"

"Yes she is, why?"

"Well, if she's not going out or anything, here soon, I'd like her to watch Rick for me, for about an hour. I'd pay her of course."

"She is going with her friends later to catch the late movie, but I'm sure she can watch Rick for a little bit."

"Much appreciated. Can she come over now?"

"I'll send her right over."

"Thanks."

4:36pm – 823 Coleman Rd.

Matthew Davenport pulled up to the King residence in his royal blue 1959 Chevy Apache. Although he saw no car in the driveway, he opted to park at the curb. Mathew exited his vehicle and walked up the driveway toward the front porch. The absence of a car worried him.

Matthew climbed up the porch steps, and was greeted by a note taped to the door. Written on it, in bold letters, was:

> **Not home tonight.**
>
> **Candy on table.**
>
> **Only one piece per child!**

Matthew looked over at the small table next to the door. On it was an orange plastic jack-o-lantern, filled with candy. Absent mindedly, he reached into it, pulled out a handful, and then dropped them back in. He bit his lip.

He decided to knock on the door anyway. He did so a few times, but no one answered. He tried peering into the front windows, but the curtains were drawn closed. He proceeded to walk around to the back of the house.

When he reached the backyard, he noticed a solitary bicycle leaning up against the wall. It was a black BMX style bike. The lettering across the frame indicated it was a "Torker." The name "Chris" was spelled across the yellow handlebar shield with stickers. Matthew passed by it, and proceeded to knock on the back door.

Again, there was no answer.

Well, they could have taken Billy and Chris out somewhere for Halloween. Didn't Jolene's folks live in Columbia? Maybe they were all down at the Town Square, helping to set things up.

Could be any number of reasons!

Still…

Matthew walked back to his car, hopped in and started it up. He pulled into the King's driveway, and then backed out into the street, facing the opposite direction from where he came. He stopped the car, and let it idle a moment.

Bit of a drive from here to Harriet Goodrich's place.

On the other hand, there will still be light outside for about another hour.

4:47pm – 1713 Fleet St.

"What are we going to do about the Halloween festival? We both volunteered to help work it. We're supposed to be up there at five. It'll look awful if we don't show," Debbie said to her husband.

"Well," Carlton put his hands on his shoulder and shook his head. "One of us has to stay here with Craig."

"I'm not. I don't think I could even look at him right now."

"Calm down. Here's what we'll do. You call Amanda, and see if she'll help out at the festival. That way they won't be shorthanded. You two drive up together, then Jeff and I can talk on the phone, and see what we can figure out to do about these boys. I think it'll be a good idea if we're all on the same page."

"What if someone asks me about what happened today?"

"Debbie, I doubt anyone even knows yet. If someone does ask about it, just tell them… that the boys thought that they were helping, and they didn't understand that the paint wouldn't wash off."

"That's a good idea. I mean they're just children. They wouldn't know that."

"Exactly. We just go on as normal, and this will all blow over."

Debbie exhaled.

"I'll get Amanda on the phone right now, and tell her what we came up with."

"Good, and tell her I'd like to talk to Jeff."

"I will." Amanda picked up the phone, and started dialing.

5:14pm – Goodrich House.

Matthew parked across the road from the Goodrich house. He couldn't shake the strange feeling that had come over him. He knew it was foolish to think that Harriet Goodrich could have done some harm to Billy Weaks. For goodness' sake, Harriet must be in her mid to late eighties, maybe even early nineties. Still, he felt that there was something odd about the whole thing, although he just couldn't quite put his finger on it.

He walked across the road and up the walkway toward the front door, admiring the Halloween decorations as he did so.

Harriet sure goes all out for Halloween, doesn't she? It looks like she made all of these herself.

When he reached the front door, he raised his hand to knock, but then opted to ring the doorbell instead. He gave the button one solid push, and then waited patiently. It was only a minute before the door opened. Harriet greeted him with her usual warm welcoming smile.

"Matt Davenport! You old rascal. Don't tell me you're out trying to scare up some candy. I thought you would have outgrown trick-or-treating by now," she jested.

"You're only as young as you feel, Harriet."

"I agree. My problem is, I haven't been *feeling* too well lately."

"Oh, hush," Matt said with a chuckle.

"What can I do for you, Matt?" she said, squinting at him.

"I just wanted to ask you something."

"Oh?"

"It seems that Rick and some of his friends were out earlier today, getting into some 'monkey shines' business. It upset a few people."

"I doubt little Rick could get into any kind of serious trouble."

"Most of it was just regular kids' stuff. However, someone says that they saw Rick and them spray painting 'Happy Halloween' all over Jake Tallman's truck."

"No!"

"Well, that's just it. Rick and the others say it wasn't them. They say at the time they were supposed to be committing the deed, they were over here looking for Billy Weaks."

Harriet pursed her lips.

"Oh?"

"Yes. From what I understand, he was helping you with some yard work today."

"Yes, that's right."

"Did you see Rick, or any other boys with him?"

"No. I can honestly say that I didn't."

"Hmm... I was hoping that you could tell me something. I had called Mrs. Weaks, but Billy wasn't there. She said he decided to spend the night at a friend's house."

"That's right. I drove Billy there myself."

"So," Matt said, "I actually stopped by the King place first. I was hoping to speak with Billy there. Problem was, the Kings left a note on the door saying they were away for the evening."

"That's right. I believe they mentioned something about driving into Columbia."

"I thought it might be something like that. But again, you didn't see Rick, or anyone else with Billy?"

"No."

"When Billy finished, you gave him a lift over to the Kings?"

"That's right."

Matthew looked around the yard.

"He didn't do too good of a job, did he?"

"Pardon?"

"Billy. He didn't do too good of a job with the yard. It looks like he raked the leaves into several piles, but only on one side of the yard. You see, the left side of the yard is much cleaner than the right side."

"He started to, but I felt so bad for having him over, doing work on Halloween, that I decided he could finish up tomorrow instead. Besides, I think the leaves look nice in the yard, with the scarecrows up and everything."

"I see."

Matthew rubbed his hand across his face.

"Well, thank you Harriet. I guess I'll try to catch up with Billy tomorrow."

"I'll let him know you were asking about him."

"Thank you, Harriet. You have a good evening now."

"I will. You do the same"

"Good night," he said, nodding.

Mathew turned and started to walk back to his car. He only had taken a few steps when he turned back around, just before Harriet had finished closing the door.

"Oh, what about his bike?"

"What?" Harriet asked.

"What about his bike? Billy's bike. Did he leave it here, or take it?"

"We took it. Had to twist the handlebars sideways to do it, but we managed to get it into my trunk."

"I see. Well thanks again Harriet."

"Good night, Matt." Harriet said, closing the door in front of her.

Mathew continued to his truck, got inside, and started it up. He looked back to the house, and could see Harriet peering out the window at him. He put the car in gear and drove off. Out of the corner of his eye, he could see Harriet stepping away from the window.

It was at this point, that he decided to circle the block, and come back again.

5:17PM – TOWN SQUARE.

The townsfolk had wasted no time in filling up the square. They knew that Margie always organized a good festival, and they were eager to sample the holiday fare, and play the traditional Halloween games.

The adults loved bobbing for apples and playing "pass the orange," while the kids enjoyed bean bag tosses and searching for hidden candy. Even the teenagers managed to have fun, despite how "uncool" some of the games were.

Amanda Chambers was handling the popcorn and caramel apple concession, and word was already spread through the attendees about how great the fresh caramel being used was. She was so busy that she had to have one of the other mother's make popcorn balls, while she dipped the apples.

Debbie Hanson was on duty at the cotton candy machine. She poured the orange colored sugar into the center, shook in some pumpkin spice, and it spun out the tastiest, most fragrant cotton candy anyone ever had.

Margie gathered people around and announced that the pumpkin carving contest would begin promptly at 5:30pm sharp, and that contestants would have exactly one hour to carve. There would be three categories: ages up to 8, then 8 to 12, then teens. Adults could carve if they wanted to, but only as an exhibition. Finally, children were required to have parental supervision, and could only use the safety tools provided.

"All right!" said Jake, clapping his hands together. "Let's pick out the pumpkins!"

Jake, Ed, and Margie began distributing the colored pumpkins to the contestants. As Jake had predicted, the fluorescent colors were a big hit. The kids scrambled to get their favorite color, but there was more than enough of each to go around.

Kurt and Audrey Carter's girl, Suzie, picked out a blue one. She said she was going to give it a frowny face because it looked sad.

Lester and Cindy Picket's boy, Owen, picked out a red one. He wanted to give it a mean face.

Hunter and Kimberly Jackson's boy, Toby, picked a yellow one. He was going to give it a smiley face.

Sydney and Anna Welling's boy, Paul, wanted an Orange one, because '"that's the color they are supposed to be." He was going to make a "regular" jack-o-lantern, but admitted he always had trouble carving their teeth.

Gus and Lisa Frank's girl, Rachael, picked a green one, because she thought it was "spooky."

Ed passed out the carving tools to everyone, and gave a short demonstration on how to use them. But before they began, he decided to set the mood, with a rousing round of his favorite Halloween song…

He started the first two lines alone, but everyone quickly joined in. The up-tempo song was always a crowd pleaser with the kids.

♪*Halloween Night, Halloween Night.*

The beasts come out on Halloween Night! ♪

♪*Halloween Night, Halloween Night.*

Step outside and get a fright! ♪

♪*Halloween Night, Halloween Night.*

The beasts come out on Halloween Night! ♪

♪*The crows sound: CAW!*

While big bears: MAW! ♪

♪*The dogs will: HOWL!*

While black cats: PROWL! ♪

♪*The snakes will: SLAY!*

While night owls: PREY! ♪

♪*And we'll all run scared 'til the light of day.*

And we'll all run scared 'til the light of day. ♪

♪Halloween Night, Halloween Night.

    The creeps come out on Halloween Night! ♪

♪Halloween Night, Halloween Night.

    Step outside and get a fright! ♪

♪Halloween Night, Halloween Night.

    The creeps come out on Halloween Night! ♪

♪The ghosts take: FLIGHT!

    While vampires: BITE! ♪

♪The banshees: BLAST!

    While witches: CAST! ♪

♪The ghouls will: SWAY!

    While werewolves: BAY! ♪

♪And we'll all run scared 'til the light of day.

And we'll all run scared 'til the light of day. ♪

♪Halloween Night, Halloween Night.

    The treats come out on Halloween Night! ♪

♪Halloween Night, Halloween Night.

    Step right up and take a bite! ♪

♪Halloween Night, Halloween Night.

    The treats come out on Halloween Night! ♪

♪The cakes will: BAKE!

    While puddings: SHAKE! ♪

♪*The nuts will: ROAST!*

Marshmallows: TOAST! ♪

♪*We'll laugh and: PLAY!*

'Til dawn's first: RAY! ♪

♪*And we'll all go home by the light of day.*

And we'll all go home by the light of day.♪

"Hurray!" Margie added at the end, applauding.

"One more time!"

5:20pm – Old Mill Rd.

The sun was setting.

Matthew parked his truck four houses down from Harriet Goodrich's home. He exited the vehicle, and made his way back to the house. He hated sneaking around like this, but something was off. There was a question nagging him in the back of his mind that he couldn't answer.

As he approached the house, he stopped and hid behind some high bushes. He looked around to make sure Harriet hadn't come outside. After surveying the area for a moment, he felt confident she hadn't. Quickly, he jogged around the side of the building to the back.

The backyard was a hodgepodge of bird feeders, weathervanes, rusty porch swings, and clothes lines. Matthew wasn't sure where to start. Carefully, he made his way through the hanging laundry, but couldn't locate what he was searching for. It wasn't behind the old tree. It wasn't around the swings, nor on either side of the building.

Keeping a watchful eye on all the back windows, he walked over to the cellar door. It was a double door with a big iron latch on the front. He took ahold of the latch and jostled it. It was heavy and solid. There was no way a young boy like Billy could open it by accident. No, he had been wrong. Everything appeared normal here. He had just let Rick's imagination run away with him.

Matthew took a long slow draw of cool air, then exhaled slowly in relief. It was time to go home. He'd stop at *Morty's* on the way back, and pick up a pecan pie for Rick and him. He would sit down with Rick and reassure him Billy was with the Kings, and was fine. Then, they would spend the rest of the evening discussing what Rick needed to do to make amends for the trouble he had caused.

He began to walk back around to the front of the house when something caught his eye. There was something sticking out of the pile of leaves next to the cellar door. Something... *blue*.

Matthew approached the leaf pile, and began to clear it. Slowly at first, but then with increasing speed. He grabbed hold of the object and lifted it up, shaking the last of the leaves off it. There had been a blue bicycle hidden underneath the leaves. He examined the frame, the handlebars, the seat, and then finally, he noticed the framed blue nameplate attached to the rear fender. It said:

/BILLY\

A shudder filled his body as he stared at it, transfixed with shock. In his hand, was the answer to his question: *Why had there been only one bike at the King house?*

Matthew dropped the bicycle, and grabbed the latch on the cellar door. He forced the latch open, then slowly, and as quietly as possible, lifted each door up, and to the side. He peered down the stairs, but it was very dark. He heard a muffled sound coming from within.

"HELmph! HELLLmph! HELLLLmph!"

Matthew took a step through the door.

"Billy?"

Scores of dark thin tentacles reached out of the blackness, and dragged him inside.

5:30pm – 1714 Fleet St.

It was sunset.

Rick paced back and forth in the living room. He couldn't believe that Tina Banes was just sitting calmly on the couch, watching TV. He stopped, looked at her and shook his head.

"It doesn't take this much time to go to the King's house and come back!"

"Your grandfather is fine, Rick. He, like, probably just stopped somewhere," she said.

"No. Something's wrong. He wouldn't be gone this long without calling and telling me. He wouldn't!"

"Rick, he's fine."

"Can you call the King's house again?"

"We've done that, like, twice already. They're probably out trick-or-treating, or at the festival."

"Look, something bad is going to happen soon. It's the truth! We've got to do something to stop it."

"Rick, go back up to your room, and calm down. I shouldn't have let you come down here to begin with. You're, like, all wound up over nothing."

"But…"

"Go!"

Rick ascended the stairs with a sigh. He opened the door to his room, and sat down at his desk. He thumbed through his copy of *Dracula*, but tossed it aside. He then reached across the desktop, and picked up the picture frame he kept there. He placed it right in front of him and studied it. It was a picture of him when he was five-years-old, surrounded by his mother and father.

Rick hopped up from his desk and looked around the room. He grabbed his almanac up off his bed, and walked to the window with it.

What had the witch said?

After sunset, when twilight was upon them…

Sunset was at 5:30pm…

But!

But his grandad had taught Rick that twilight and sunset are not the same things…

Let's see…

There was nautical twilight, but why would a witch go by that?

No…

Astronomical twilight! That would be it!

Rick started skimming through the almanac.

Astronomical twilight was going to be at 6:55pm.

There was still enough time!

Rick opened his closet door, reached in, and picked up his signal flashlight. He walked back to the window, opened it up, kneeled on the chest resting beneath the sill, then reached the flashlight out the window, and pointed it at Craig's house. He began flashing it quickly, hoping to get Craig's attention. After a moment, Rick saw several quick flashes coming from Craig's window in response. He then began his message:

--. .-. .- -. -.. .- -.. / --. --- -. . . / .-- . / -- ..- ... - / ... .- ...- . / - --- .-- -.

Craig replied:

.... --- .--

Rick:

... -. . . .- -.- / --- ..- - / .-. .. -.. . / - --- / -- . --- --- -.. . - . .. -.-. .... / ..- -. .- .. . / -... .. .-.. .-.. -.--

Craig:

... ..- -. .... . - / .- .-.. .-. . .- -.. -.--

Rick:

- .-- .. .-. .. .. --. .... - / -. --- - / ..- -. . - .. .-.. / ... .. -..- / ..-. .. ..-. - -.-- / ..-. .. ...- .

Craig:

--- -.- / -- . . - / .- - / .-. --- -... .---- . .... / ..-. .. ...- . / - .. -. ..- - - . .... / -... .-. .. .. -. --. / -- .- ... -.- ...

Rick:

.-- .... -.-- / -- .- ... -.- ...

94

Craig:

... --- / .- -.. ..- .-.. - ... / .-- --- -. .----. - / .-. . -.-. --- --. -. .. --.. . / ..- ...

Rick:

--- -.- / --- ...- . .-.

Craig:

--- ...- . .-.

Rick stepped away from the window. He opened his school backpack, and placed the flashlight inside. He also dug up his Swiss Army Knife from his nightstand drawer, and tossed it in as well. He reached under his bed, and pulled out the box with his Halloween costume in it.

The cardboard box was brightly colored and featured a transparent top, so that you could see the set's mask inside. Printed on the box in friendly letters was the manufacturer's logo: "Ben Cooper." Across the box it also read "Dracula." Rick took the top off the box, and removed the mask. The set also included a vinyl suit, and an inflatable bird that attached to the shoulder, but he saw no need for those under the circumstances. He placed the mask into his backpack, and zipped it shut.

In the house across the street, Craig slowly opened his bedroom door, and crossed the hall to the guest room. He opened the guest room's side window, and stuck his head out. The drain pipe was just outside the window, to the right. Craig tossed his mask down to the ground, slid his left leg out the window, and kept his right arm pressed against the interior wall. He stretched his left arm out, and grabbed hold of the pipe. His slid more of his body out of the window, his right hand keeping a firm hold of the frame. He then planted his feet against the exterior wall, released the window frame, and grabbed hold of the drain pipe with his right hand. He then made his way down the pipe, letting himself drop the last six or seven feet. Craig picked up his mask, then made his way to the front porch, retrieved his bike, and rode down to Rob's house. He found Rick waiting on him.

"How did you get here so fast?" Craig asked.

"My grandad makes me keep a rope ladder in my room in case of a fire. I just hooked it on the window, and climbed down."

"I gotta get me one of those."

"'*Learn not to burn*,'" Rick replied with a smile.

Craig chuckled, then reached down and picked up a small rock. With a practiced hand, he tossed it up to Rob's window, to get his attention. When Rob didn't immediately show up at the window, Craig tossed another rock. This time Rob came over and opened the window.

"What's goin' on?"

"Rob, we have to go to Miss Goodrich's and help Billy," answered Rick

"We can't go over there."

"We have to. We're the only ones that know what's going on. Besides, my grandad was supposed to go to the King's to see if Billy was there, and he hasn't come back yet. If he went to Miss Goodrich's house as well, he could be in trouble. We've got to help him."

"But what can *we* do?"

"We just sneak in through the cellar door, and untie Billy. If Grandpa Matt is there, we untie him too, and then we leave."

"I don't know."

"What if it was you?"

"Ok, I'm comin' down."

"Bring your Halloween mask," added Craig.

"Why?"

"To use it as a disguise. That way the sheriff, or anybody that sees us, won't recognize us. Besides, it's Halloween, if you wear a monster's mask, you get their power. Everyone knows that."

"I wish."

Rob retrieved his mask, and tossed it out the window. Craig deftly caught it. Rob then lowered himself out the bedroom window onto the wooden porch awning. He walked down the awning, grabbed hold of its edge, and dropped down to the porch railing. He then simply hopped down to the ground.

"I don't know why parents always send us kids to our rooms," Craig intoned. "We always have a way to get out."

"We had better hurry before they notice we're gone."

"Right. Here's your mask Rob."

"Thanks."

Rob got on his bike, and pulled his mask down over his face. It was a mask of Frankenstein's monster.

Rick retrieved the Dracula mask from his back pack, and put it on.

"Who do you have?" Rick asked Craig.

"Are you kidding me?" Craig unhooked his mask from his bicycle handles, and put it on. "Your *Dracula*, he's *Frankenstein*... I'm the *Werewolf*."

Craig put on his "Hairy and Scary" Werewolf mask, with shaggy fake hair rooted to it. He then climbed onto his bike.

"Let's ride!"

The boys rode off, into the night.

5:56PM – TOWN SQUARE.

At the pavilion, Margie Sutter called out to remind the contestants:

"Attention everyone, you only have about thirty minutes to finish up carving your jack-o-lanterns. We're going to announce the winner at 6:45 sharp, so we can move on to the costume parade, and get it finished up by 7:30!"

"Thanks Margie!"

"Thank you, Mrs. Sutter!"

"Thanks!"

Amanda Hanson made her way from the caramel apple stand, over to Margie.

"Margie, we're running out of popcorn. Is there some more we can make?"

"Yes dear, Edgar has some more in the back of his truck. He has one of those hot air poppers. Just plug it in and it'll be ready in no time."

"I don't know how you do it Margie."

"Do what?"

"Every year, you run this festival, keep things moving along, and manage to put up with all the kids. I think it would drive me crazy."

"It's not that difficult dealing with kids. Not really. I find that the secret is just to listen to them. Most of the time, if a child is anxious, it's because they feel they have something important to say to you. Oh, it may be about something you find inconsequential, but it's important to them. So, the best thing to do is listen."

"Usually when Rob is trying to tell me something, I just let it go in one ear and out the other. Maybe that's why I have trouble with him sometimes."

"We forget that young people are just that… young 'people'. They have their own feelings and their own thoughts. If we treat them with a little respect, they'll do the same for us."

"Thank you, Margie." Amanda smiled. "I should probably get busy making the rest of that popcorn."

"Anytime Amanda," she replied. "Be sure to save one of those caramel balls for me."

"I will."

Down the road, the boys rode up and approached Town Square. They stopped short of the pavilion, and watched as the townspeople played games and carved pumpkins. Rob and Craig spotted their mothers helping with the festivities. They also saw Tanner and Driscoe crossing the street toward the 7-Eleven.

"Uh-oh," yelped Rob.

"Don't worry about it. We just keep our masks on, and we ride past them like everything is normal. No one will even notice," Craig instructed.

"Ok."

The trio pedaled their bikes casually past the pavilion. They could hear Tanner and Driscoe talking as they rode by:

"What are we doing?"

"We're going to the store, and pick up a carton of eggs."

"Why?" Tanner stopped in the middle of the road, and turned to Driscoe. "Later, we'll go by and 'egg' Mr. Williams' house. He'll probably blame it on Craig and his loser friends."

"That's a good one, Tanner!"

When the boys had ridden past the bullies, Rob whispered over to Craig

"That's not fair!"

"We can't do anything about it now. Just keep going."

"It's still not fair."

The boys continued on past the 7-Eleven, ignoring Tanner and Driscoe. When they reached Harvest Rd, they turned right and continued on toward Old Mill Rd.

6:28pm – Old Mill Rd.

The three friends made their way north up Old Mill Rd, and stopped within viewing distance of the Goodrich house. The once festive scarecrows and dangling ghosts now appeared dark and ominous. The boys could see Harriet, on her porch, setting out candies and treats on a folding table she had set up. Rick noticed she was now placing out apples.

"What if she put a spell on those apples, or something?" he asked.

"Why would she?" Craig replied.

"She's a witch. They put spells on apples. It's what they do."

"Good point."

Craig looked down the street and saw groups of young Trick-or-Treaters making their way down the street, one house at a time.

"We have to stop anyone from going trick-or-treating at her house."

"How we gonna do that?" asked Rob.

Craig lifted up his mask for a moment, and let it rest on the top of his head. He ran his fingers across his mouth.

"I don't know."

"I wish we could get the police up here," said Rick.

"We can't. Even if we did call them, they wouldn't listen to us," said Rob.

Craig peered over his shoulder at Rob.

"But we do know someone they *will* listen to."

"Who?' Rick asked.

"That old man, Hoyt Williams."

"He ain't gonna help us!" Rob said firmly.

"He will, if he doesn't *know* that he's helping us."

"Huh?"

"What do you mean?"

"We trick him into calling the police for us."

"How we gonna do that?"

Craig smiled.

"By acting like Tanner Blake."

Craig, Rob, and Rick stood at the edge of the Williams' house. They examined the darkened building. The curtains had been drawn shut to conceal any light inside. It was devoid of any holiday decorations, not even a jack-o-lantern. Even the porchlight was off.

Craig inhaled.

"Get ready," he said.

"With pleasure," said Rob.

"Remember, just aim for his door," added Rick.

"Ok, one, two, three, go!"

The boys began pelting the Williams' porch and door with small rocks they had hastily gathered from neighboring yards. They then began chanting loudly:

♫ *"Trick or treat?!*

Up the street!

We're the monsters that you'll meet! ♫

♫ *If you do,*

Just beware,

We'll give you a shocking scare!" ♫

♫ *Shock-ing-scare!*

Shock-ing scare!" ♫

"Keep going!" said Craig.

♫ *"Trick or treat?!*

Smell my feet!

Give me something good to eat! ♫

♫ *If you don't,*

Then it's fair,

I'll pull down your underwear! ♫

♫ *Un-der-wear!*

Un-der-wear!" ♫

    It wasn't long before Hoyt Williams came bursting out of the front door. He was having quite a fit.

"You kids! You stop it right now!" he demanded.

"No way, old man!" yelled Craig.

"Yeah!" added Rob.

The boys continued throwing small rocks at the porch.

♫ *"Trick or treat?!*

Don't you cheat!

I need something good and sweet!" ♫

"I said stop it!" he shouted again.

♫ *"If it's not,*

You'll despair,

I'll toss flour at your hair! ♫

♫ *At-your-hair!*

At-your-hair!" ♫

"I'm calling the sheriff on you heathens!"

"Go on! We're not afraid of him!" replied Craig.

♫ *"Trick or treat?!*

It's so neat!

Feed the ghosties in the sheet! ♫

♪ *Tell us no,*

If you dare,

We'll go haunt you everywhere! ♪

♪ *Eve-ry-where!*

Eve-ry-where!

We're eve-ry-where… ♪

Boo!"

Hoyt spun around to go back inside. When he did, Craig said, in a purposely loud voice:

 "C'mon! Let's go *egg* the Goodrich house!"

"Yeah!"

"Yes! Let us *egg* the *Goodrich* house!"

Hoyt ran inside the house and picked up the telephone from the hall table. He lifted the handset to his head, and began dialing numbers.

"Hello? Sheriff?! Sheriff?!!"

The boys could hear him yelling from inside the house. They then dropped their remaining supply of rocks, hopped on their seats, and rode off, up the street.

6:32PM – 1713 FLEET ST.

Carlton Chambers walked up the stairs to his son's room. He knocked on the door. When there was no response, he knocked again.

"Son? Son I want to talk to you."

Carlton turned the knob, and swung the door open.

"Craig?"

Carlton was surprised to find the room empty. He checked the upstairs bathroom, but there was no light coming from under the door. He knocked on it, then opened it. Still no Craig. He checked the guest room, but it too was empty. That's when he noticed the guestroom window was open. He stuck his head through the open window, looked around, and then called out:

"Craig?"

When he received no response, he shut the window and ran down the stairs. Quickly, he checked the downstairs bathroom, and kitchen. He then picked up the telephone and called Jeff Hanson.

"Jeff? Sorry to bug you again. Can you check to see if Rob is in his room?" He asked. "Why? Because Craig's not in his… Ok… I'll wait."

Carlton hung onto the phone anxiously, awaiting Jeff to get back to him. It only took a minute.

"Well, they could be anywhere… No, I don't think they'd go over there… I'll run over and ask Mr. Davenport… If they're not there we'll just have to drive around and look for them… Ok…Ok… Be over soon."

Carlton hung up the phone, grabbed his coat and car keys, and ran out the door.

6:34pm – Goodrich House.

In her kitchen, Harriet lit a wooden torch. She then opened the cellar door, and slowly walked down the stairs. To her delight, each step creaked and groaned as she did so. When she reached the bottom of the stairs, she smiled at her captives.

"Hello, my pretties," she said, laughing at herself.

"HELmph! HELLLmph! HELLLLmph!"

"Yes, yes. 'Help, help, help!' Don't you ever get tired of calling for 'help'? A smart boy would have given up long ago. At least you're not crying for your mommy, I suppose," she growled.

"Youf leav tphat boyf alom!" came another muffled voice.

Harriet walked over to her other prisoner, and leered down at him.

"I'll do whatever I please, Mr. Davenport!"

A gagged Matt Davenport was sitting in the corner of the cellar. His hands were tied behind his back. His feet were also bound together. There was a visible bruise on his forehead.

"I knew you'd be trouble the moment you came to the door. I never saw it in you before, but tonight, in the *Hallow'eve* light, I did," she said rubbing her free hand through his hair. "I saw it glimmering in your eye. You were touched by the supernatural long ago, probably as a child. That's why deep inside, you suspected the truth. That's why I waited for you to come back."

Harriet then walked to each of the torches on either side of the well, and lit them. When she did, the fire created exploded with sparks. She then dowsed the torch she was holding in a barrel of water that sat in the opposite corner of the cellar.

"Of course, in the end, it doesn't really matter if you came back or went home. In nineteen minutes, I'm going to open the portal in the well, and change this world forever."

"Did you hear that? Nineteen minutes!" Craig said.

The three boys were all crouched outside the cellar window, masks up, looking in. They all stood-up, and pressed their bodies against the outer wall, hoping to avoid detection.

"What are we gonna do?"

"We have to lure her out of the cellar. But how?" asked Rick.

"It's Halloween," Craig said, "it's about time we did some 'doorbell ditching'."

"Huh?"

"Rick, you run up to the front, then start ringing her doorbell like crazy. Rob, you go up with him, but hide around the front corner, so you can see both of us. When old lady Goodrich leaves the cellar, I'll signal you, and then you call to Rick. Then both of you come running around to the back. We all force open the cellar door, and get Billy and your grandpa out."

"Why do *I* have to go up front?"

"Because you're the fastest runner."

"We ain't gonna have enough time to get them both untied," said Rob.

"Sure we are. We just need to untie their legs so they can run. We can untie their hands when we get away."

"Here, take this," Rick said. He reached into his backpack, pulled out his Swiss Army Knife, and handed it to Craig.

"Great. Thanks, Rick."

"Sure."

"Ok, masks down."

The boys pulled their masks back down over their faces.

"Go!"

Rick ran around to the front of the house as fast as he could. He stepped gingerly up the stairs, then turned to face the corner he had just come around.

Rob trotted up just behind Rick. When he reached the corner of the house, he peeked around it carefully, placing his hands on the building for support. He glanced back at Craig.

Craig kneeled down in front of the cellar window. He lowered his head all the way to the ground so he could look inside. He then gave a 'thumbs up" to Rob.

Rob in turn, looked at Rick, and forwarded the 'thumbs up" to him.

Rick took a deep breath, and began jamming the doorbell button with his thumb.

Ring

RingRing

RingRingRing

RingRingRingRing

"You would think those brats would be happy with the treats I left them on the porch," Harriet hissed.

Ring

RingRing

RingRingRing

RingRingRingRing

"Aaaaagh," she seethed.

Ring

RingRing

RingRingRing

RingRingRingRing

"Go away!"

Ring

RingRing

RingRingRing

RingRingRingRing

She began pacing around the cellar.

Ring

RingRing

RingRingRing

RingRingRingRing

"Fine, you little cretins!"

Ring

RingRing

RingRingRing

RingRingRingRing

Harriet stormed up the stairs into the kitchen.

Ring

RingRing

RingRingRing

RingRingRingRing

Craig popped up, and waved like mad to Rob, motioning him to come.

Rob whistled at Rick, and did the same.

Rick jumped off the porch and started to run. As he turned the front corner, he saw Rob running to the backyard as well. He sped past the cellar window, and took a sharp turn around the back corner of the house. When he did, he saw that Craig and Rob were already pushing the latch on the cellar door up. Each grabbed one of the double doors, and swung them open.

"Hurry!" said Craig.

The boys piled down the cellar steps.

Rick ran right up to his grandad, and pulled the gag down from his mouth. He began working on the rope around his grandad's ankles.

"Don't worry grandpa, we're getting you out of here."

"Rick? What are you doing here?"

"Shhh! I'm saving you!"

Rob ran up the cellar stairs and put his ear against the kitchen door.

"I don't hear anything."

Craig pulled down Billy's gag, and immediately started to try to untie the ropes binding the boy's feet.

"Hurry! Please!" Billy said.

"I can't figure out this knot!"

Craig flicked open Rick's pocket knife, and began cutting through the ropes.

"Rick, you have to get out of here, now!" pleaded Matt.

"No. I'm not leaving you here."

Rick pulled at the knot several different ways, and started to feel it loosen.

Craig cut through the rope around Billy's ankles.

Rick untied the knot around his grandad's ankles.

"Let's go!" Craig called to Rob in a hushed tone.

Rob scrambled down the stairs and joined the others. Together, they made their way to the cellar steps leading up to the backyard.

Harriet was waiting for them at the top.

"Eeeeh-hee-hee-hee-hee-heeee!"

The group below froze in their tracks.

"You didn't think that you'd get away from me, did you?" she shrieked. "There will be no escape! I've waited too long for this!"

Then in the distance…

Weeee-oooooo, Weeee-oooooo!

Weeee-oooooo, Weeee-oooooo!

…the boys heard the rhythmic wail of the approaching police siren.

Weeee-oooooo, Weeee-oooooo!

Weeee-oooooo, Weeee-oooooo!

"It's over you witch!" exclaimed Rick. "The police are on their way here right now!"

"You're beaten!" added Craig.

"Yeah!"

"Eeeeh-hee-hee-hee-hee-heeee!"

"Eeeeh-hee-hee-hee-hee-heeee!"

"Beaten? Beaten? **BEATEN???**"

Harriet's right leg suddenly grew over a foot in length, causing her body to slouch to the left.

"Do you think you can defeat me? I, who have battled the Atomic Knights of Graph, beaten?"

Her shoulders widened.

"I, who defeated the Feathered Physicist of Zen, beaten?"

Her arms lengthened.

"Do you think I am not prepared?"

Her gnarled hand reached up to her face. She dug her now blackened fingernails up under her chin. Harriet pulled her human face off, like a Halloween mask, revealing a crimson scaly skin. She pointed a boney finger at the kids.

"Your Child Magic is no match for my Dark Arts!"

Her left leg grew to match her right one. Both of her knees made a cracking sound, and then folded in backwards. Cloven hooves burst forth out of both of her shoes.

"Now, you will all tremble before me!"

Her torso extended slightly as she bent forward, a hunch growing on her back like an inflating balloon. Her white hair grew into a hundred-thousand long black strands that danced around her head like winding snakes, each one seemingly with a life of its own.

"Behold, the Red Witch of Andromeda!"

"Eeeeh-hee-hee-hee-hee-heeee!"

"Now, Earth Children, you will *all* go down the well!"

"Get away from them, you hag!" Matt Davenport yelled as he charged at the Red Witch.

The Red Witch hissed at him. Her serpentine hair shot forward, grabbed a hold of Matt, and flung him across the room, into the cellar wall. He landed on the floor, unconscious.

"Eeeeh-hee-hee-hee-hee-heeee!"

"Grandpa!"

The Red Witch's hair shot out across the room like lightning, wrapping itself around all of the boys. It then lifted them high off the ground, where they hung helplessly, like flies caught in a spider's web. They all struggled to break free, but it was no use.

Weeee-oooooo, Weeee-oooooo!

Weeee-oooooo, Weeee-oooooo!

Weeee-oooooo, Weeee-oooooo!

Weeee-oooooo, Weeee-oooooo!

"Do you hear that pizza face? That's the police. They have guns, they can stop you!" quipped Craig.

"Nothing can stop me now!" she screamed. As she did she raised her arms into the air. "Rise up my minions! Rise up and fight!"

With that, the flames of the two torches flanking the well roared high into the air, each turning bright orange-pink.

6:40PM – TOWN SQUARE.

Underneath the canopy of the Town Square pavilion, the Jack-o-Lanterns began to shake. Sparks started to fly out of the electrical wiring and bulb sockets. Margie Sutter cried out.

"Jake! What's going on?"

"I don't know, Margie!"

Jake and Edgar ran over to their friend. More sparks exploded forth from the electrical system. Then all the lights in Town Square began to shake.

The stop lights blew out!

Ka-plow!

The street lamps blew out!

Ka-plow!

All the fluorescent bulbs, in all the shops blew out!

Ka-Boom!

The festival-goers were left in darkness. People started to scramble in panic.

"It's ok everyone!" Jake said to calm the crowd.

"It's probably just some type of electrical surge," added Edgar.

"There's nothing to be worried about!"

Margie stared quizzically in the direction of the pavilion.

"Jake," she asked, softly, "I thought it was those special bulbs that made the jack-o-lanterns light up like that?"

"It is," he reassured her.

"Then why are they all still glowing?"

Both Jake and Edgar turned to face the jack-o-lanterns. Even without the ultra-violet light, they all glowed brightly.

The candle in *Suzie Carter's* frowning blue jack-o-lantern lit up with a bright orange-pink flame.

The candle in *Owen Picket's* sinister red jack-o-lantern lit up with a bright orange-pink flame.

The candle in *Toby Jackson's* smiling yellow jack-o-lantern lit up with a bright orange-pink flame.

The candle in *Paul Welling's* toothless orange jack-o-lantern lit up with a bright orange-pink flame.

The candle in *Racheal Frank's* spooky green jack-o-lantern lit up with a bright orange-pink flame.

Then, one-by-one, all the other jack-o-lanterns lit-up with the mysterious fire.

"What in heaven's name?" Margie muttered.

Suddenly, all the jack-o-lanterns sprung to life, and with evil glee, began hopping through the air towards the townspeople.

"Aaaaaaaagh!!!!!!!"

6:40pm – Old Mill Rd.

Sherriff Wilson pulled his car up to the Goodrich house with a screech. He and Deputy Reynolds flung their doors open, and jumped out. A concerned parent, out trick-or-treating with her daughter, called out to them.

"Josh? Greg? Is everything ok?" asked Mrs. Small.

"Hi, Lydia," Sherriff Wilson answered. "We got a call down at the station that a bunch of kids were running around out here, throwing rocks at people and houses."

"Have you seen anything?" asked the deputy.

"No. Not at all. Everything has been real quiet," she replied.

"We were told they might be headed over here to Miss Goodrich's. You should keep Megan on the other side of the street for right now."

"I will Sheriff."

The squad car started to shake violently. The horn started blaring on it.

"What the…?"

Then all of the cars up and down the street started to shake. Their horns too began to sound. People hurried outside of their homes to check on the commotion.

The squad car's cherry lights blew apart. Porch lights exploded, followed by the lights within people's homes. The sound of frightened screams filled the air.

"Sherriff, what's going on?"

"I don't know! Greg, see if you can grab the bullhorn, and start telling everyone to come outside for safety. These explosions could set the neighborhood on fire!"

"Right, Sherriff!"

Greg Reynolds reached into the quaking car through the window, and managed to grab hold of the bullhorn. He turned it on and began calling out to the neighborhood's citizens.

"Everyone, this is Deputy Greg Reynolds! For your own safety, we need everyone to exit their homes! There is some type of electrical disturbance on this street, and we feel it may pose a fire hazard! Please exit your homes in a calm and orderly manner!"

People began leaving their yards, and crossing the street toward the Sherriff. They congregated in the middle of the road, in front of the Goodrich house.

"Now folks," Sherriff Wilson said, "I just need everyone to keep their cool. I'm sure we'll all be fine. There's probably a simple explanation for all of this."

Lydia Small pointed toward the Goodrich farm.

"But what about for those?"

The crowd looked up and gasped. The scarecrows were rattling loudly on their posts. Their arms and legs flailed madly. The candles inside them lit up by themselves. Then tall jets of flame shot out from the tops of their heads.

Ka-shoom!

Lydia screamed like Janet Leigh.

"WHAT'S HAPPENING??!?!?!?!"

Megan Small flipped up her bunny mask and exclaimed:

"Halloween! That's what's happening!"

The scarecrows leapt off their perches, grew long stilt-like legs, and began striding towards the families gathered in the street, swinging their iron-clawed hands as they moved.

6:46PM – TOWN SQUARE.

Town Square was in total chaos. The animated jack-o-lanterns flew around everywhere. Seemingly invulnerable, they smashed through solid objects without a care. They hurled themselves at people, knocking their victims to the ground.

A yellow 'rambler' ricocheted itself into the posts supporting the pavilion.

Wooga-Booga! Woooga-Booga!

The damage caused the whole structure to collapse.

An orange 'flamer' then came by and spit fire on the rubble.

Kaaaa-flooooosh!

Igniting the remains of the pavilion into a giant bonfire.

Five red 'howlers' banded together in a pack.

Aaah-oooh! Aaah-ooooooooh!

They chased a young girl, dressed as a cat, across the central fairground, and up a tree. They kept bouncing up and down, nipping at her heels, all the while baying at the moon.

Aaah-oooh! Aaah-ooooooooh!

A blue 'chomper' attacked the concession stands.

Yump-yump, yump-yump!

It started smashing them to pieces to get at the candy apples and hot dogs. Several more joined together and smashed through the window of *Morty's Diner*, and began a feeding frenzy.

Yump-yump, yump-yump!

Yump-yump, yump-yump!

Edgar Porter was trying to get to his truck when a green 'wailer' landed in front of him. Edgar stopped dead in his tracks out of fright. The wailer leaped into the air, and emitted an ear shattering cry that caused the windshield of Edgar's car to shatter.

Waaaaaiiiiiiiiiiiiih!!!!!!

Then a rambler landed on the truck's hood, and bounced up and down, smashing the engine to pieces. Edgar turned and ran in the other direction, trying to find some means of escape.

Wooga-Booga! Wooooga-Booga!

Margie and Jake started to herd families toward the cinema.

"Everyone! Get inside the movie house! The walls are solid, and we can lock up the theatre doors!" Jake called out.

"Hurry! Hurry!"

"Everyone, quickly!"

Several orange flamers zoomed past the duo, and crashed through the theatres glass front. They floated in the air, and began to spin in circles, fire spewing from their mouths like molten lava. The cinema lobby was quickly engulfed in flames.

Kaaaa-flooooosh!

Kaaaa-flooooosh!

Tanner and Driscoe cowered in the 7-Eleven. They crawled down the aisles on their hands and knees.

"What are we gonna do, Tanner?"

"They have a walk-in freezer in the back. It's made of steel. We can hide in it."

They moved across the floor towards the refrigerated section; when they reached it, they came face to face with a yellow rambler.

"Uh-oh."

The yellow rambler, smiled at them.

Wooga-Booga! Wooooga-Booga!

"Run!"

The teens hopped to their feet and headed toward the front door. The rambler chased after them, bouncing from the floor to the ceiling to the walls as it did, leveling the interior of the store. Relentlessly, it continued to pursue them around the square, until they ran to the back of the cinema, and dived into its dumpster.

Wooga-Booga! Wooooga-Booga!

Amanda Hanson and Debbie Chambers had picked up two of the smaller children, and were carrying them in their arms.

"Get to the car! Get to the car!" cried Debbie.

"We've got to get out of here!"

Relentlessly, they raced to the vehicle. As they approached it, they were astonished to see a group of blue chompers begin to devour it, bite by bite.

Yump-yump, yump-yump!

Yump-yump, yump-yump!

"What are we going to do?"

"I don't know!" screamed Debbie.

Waaaaaiiiiiiiiiiiiih!!!!!!

6:46PM – OLD MILL RD.

Both the 'burlap' scarecrows and the 'pumpkin' scarecrows moved quickly. Their long legs made it easy for them to chase down people. Seeing the children as no threat, they picked adults as their primary targets, and pursued them without reservation.

One of the pumpkin scarecrows engaged Sherriff Wilson directly. It swung at him with its rake and maul hands, trying to strike him across the chest, roaring as it attacked.

Ahhroooooor!

The Sherriff was able to block a few of the things with his baton, but received a cut on his right shoulder. He ducked under a few more swings, and tried to put the squad car between him and his foe.

When the scarecrow followed him, Sherriff Wilson circled around to the other side of the car. Frustrated, the creature stepped up onto the car top and swung feverishly at him. Knowing he had a clean shot, the Sherriff drew his revolver, and squeezed the trigger twice.

Blam!

Blam!

The bullets hit their mark, blowing two holes in the scarecrow's head. It staggered a bit, but then regained its footing. Helplessly, the Sherriff watched as the two fresh holes sealed themselves shut. The creature smiled a fiendish smile, and chuckled.

Wha-ha-ha-ha!

Deputy Reynolds fared no better. The burlap scarecrows were just as aggressive as their cohorts. The one attacking him clawed at him fiercely, like a wild animal. The deputy avoided a flurry of strikes, and managed to land a solid blow against its head. The scarecrow spun in place on one leg, like a top. When it stopped spinning, it quickly regained a solid stance, and came after him again.

Ahhroooooor!

Lydia Small carried her child over her shoulder as she ran down the street, another pumpkin scarecrow in pursuit. The creature was gaining on her quickly. She screamed aloud. The fiend raised its sickle-shaped hand high in the air, ready to strike.

Ahhrooooor!

"Over here! Over here!" a voice called out to her.

Instinctively, she followed the sound of the voice. She ran into a nearby yard, Megan still in tow, and saw Hoyt Williams on the porch, waving her on.

"Hurry! Get inside! Get upstairs!"

She ran up the porch steps, past Hoyt, through his front doorway, and straight up the stairs. The beast seamlessly turned its focus on Hoyt, and moved within striking distance.

"Batter up!" he yelled, slamming his bat into the monsters belly!

The bat shattered, as the scarecrow hunched over.

Ahhrooooor!

"Holy cow!"

Hoyt lost no time in spinning around, and franticly following Lydia up the stairs. When he reached the top, he pulled the attic door down from the ceiling, and extended the ladder.

"Climb up! Climb up!" he urged Lydia.

"Hurry, Megan, hurry!" she said lifting Megan unto the ladder. When Megan was in the attic, she followed, then Hoyt.

The scarecrow pushed the door open and ran up the stairs. Hoyt pulled the attic door shut, just before the monster reached the top of the flight. The scarecrow then began to hack away at the door, attempting to get at its prey.

Ahhroooooor!

Ahhroooooor!

6:51PM – GOODRICH HOUSE.

The Red Witch cackled once more.

"Eeeeh-hee-hee-hee-hee-heeee!"

"The time is at hand! In mere minutes I will use your Child Magic to open the portal, at let my coven loose upon your world!

"You won't get away with this you smelly old hag!" yelled Craig.

"Yeah, smelly!"

"But I already am getting away with it. I already am!" she laughed.

"Eeeeh-hee-hee-hee-hee-heeee!"

"I'm going to stop you!" shouted Rick.

"Stop me? I am the Red Witch," she spat. "I am the terror of the Black Mountains. The scourge of Taurus Four. Who do you think you are that can stop me? Who do any of you think you are?"

"I'm…"

Rick looked at his friends, they too twisted and turned, tangled in the Red Witch's hair.

"I'm…"

Rick looked at his grandfather lying helpless on the floor.

"I'm…"

"Eeeeh-hee-hee-hee-hee-heeee!"

Rick looked and saw himself, in a standing mirror leaning against the wall, and realized he was still wearing his mask.

"It's Halloween," he called to Craig and Rob. "That means if you wear a monster's mask, you have their powers! Everyone knows that!" He turned to the Red Witch, and proclaimed:

"I'm *Dracula!* And Dracula… can change to… SMOKE!"

Poof

Rick turned into a stream of smoke, and flew out of the witch's grasp.

"Noooooo!" she cried.

Poof

Rick materialized, standing on the cellar floor. The Red Witch screamed and commanded her hair to dart after him.

Poof

The sinister tendrils missed their mark, finding only vapor instead.

Inspired, Rob took a deep breath and yelled:

"I'm *Frankenstein!* And Frankenstein is STRONG!" Grunting, he flexed his arms, and tore the witch's hair away from his body, breaking free from her clutches.

"Rrrraaarrrr!"

The Red Witch howled in pain.

Rob charged her, and with a mighty shove, threw her against the wall! The shock caused her to groan in pain, and drop Craig and Billy from her grasp. Billy ran behind some old furniture. Craig stood up.

"I'm the *Werewolf!*" he shouted. "And the Werewolf is FAST!"

Craig snarled. He pounced on the Red Witch like lightning, landing on top of her, and knocking her to the ground! He then leapt off her, and started leaping around the room, on all fours.

"Grrrrr!"

The Red Witch got back on her feet. She tried to re-capture the boys with her tentacle hair, but it was a futile attempt. Rick would just keep turning into smoke. Rob kept ripping her hair apart, and Craig was just too quick and spry.

"I'll destroy you all!" she yelled in frustration.

"Don't think so, lady!" Craig said, running circles around her. "Grrrrr!"

Rick materialized in front of her.

"You'd have to catch us first," he said.

The Red Witch swung at him, trying to claw him with her hands. Rick simply disappeared.

Poof

He then re-appeared somewhere else.

Poof

"And you don't seem to be able to do that," he added.

Rob roared. He grabbed an old storage chest, and threw it at her. It broke over her back, causing her to stagger.

"Rrrraaarrrr!"

"Stop it, you brats!" she ordered.

Poof

"I don't think so."

Poof

The witch started swinging her arms wildly, trying to strike at Rick. The more he avoided her assault, the angrier she became.

"You're ruining everything!"

Poof

Rick materialized, standing on the edge of the well.

"Too bad, so sad," he chided.

With a visceral yell of contempt, she lurched at him, swinging wide. As she did, Craig leapt at her feet.

Poof

The witch struck air.

"Rrrraaarrrr!"

Rob shoved her hard in the back.

"Grrrrr!"

She stumbled over Craig,

        and

        fell

        down

        the

        well

"Aaaaaagggghhhhh!"

THUD!

6:55PM – TOWN SQUARE.

Every jack-o-lantern stopped.

Every yellow rambler halted bouncing.

Every orange flamer ceased spewing fire.

Every red howler gave up the chase.

Every blue chomper quit eating.

Every green wailer was silenced.

Each fell to the ground, lifeless.

The fires they had started, faded away.

It took a moment before the townspeople realized what had happened. Those that were running stopped, and just looked around at each other. Those that were in hiding peeked their heads out, and hesitantly came out from their cover.

Margie Sutter walked up to a dead green wailer, regarded it for a moment, and then kicked it as hard as she could.

"Next year, I think we'll skip the carving contest."

Jake Tallman laughed, then kicked one himself. Edgar Porter ran up and kicked the same one to Margie. She, in turn, kicked it back.

Everyone else joined in and began kicking the jack-o-lanterns around as if it was a sport. Some kicked them back and forth to each other, some tried to kick them between two trees, like they were goal posts.

Tanner and Driscoe crawled out of the trash dumpster they had been hiding in. They were covered in various refuse, from rotten banana peels, to old socks, to unidentifiable sludge. Tanner had a crushed egg all over his face and head.

"This is gross," said Driscoe.

"We're gonna stink for weeks."

Jeff and Carlton pulled up to the square in their car. Their wives ran over to meet them. When the car stopped, both men got out, and looked around at the ruin. They then noticed that everyone was kicking jack-o-lanterns all over the place. Jeff looked at his wife.

"Amanda, what's going on?"

"Honey, you wouldn't believe me if I told you."

6:55PM – OLD MILL RD.

All the scarecrows collapsed right where they stood. All their human prey froze in their tracks for a moment.

The Sherriff took his baton, and poked one a few times.

The Deputy pulled his gun, and shot the one that had been after him, just to be sure it was dead.

Hoyt Williams looked through the hole in the attic door that his pursuer had hacked open. He saw that it was just an inanimate pile on the floor.

"Is it gone?" asked Lydia.

"I think it's dead," he answered. "Or rather... *deader*."

Lydia laughed at that.

Megan looked up at her mother.

"Mom," she said sheepishly. "I don't want to do anymore trick-or-treating tonight."

Lydia embraced her daughter.

6:55PM – GOODRICH HOUSE.

The boys ran to the well, and looked down it.

"Is that it?" asked Rob.

"I think so," said Rick.

"We did it!" exclaimed Craig. "We did it. We saved the day."

"Yeah, we're heroes!"

"Just like the Three Musketeers!" added Rick.

"That's right! *One for all*," Craig said, taking his mask off and raising it high in the air, like a sword.

The other two boys followed him in suit. The trio touched their mask together and exclaimed:

"And all for one!!!"

Kaaa-looooosh!!!!

A blinding pillar of ethereal fire shot up from within the well. It consumed the masks in a flash of light and smoke.

"What the…?"

The boys looked down the well. A twisted spectral visage was flying up from the bottom. It was a terrifying apparition whose translucent form glowed brightly in an otherworldly color.

"*Eeeh-*

hee-

hee-

hee-

hee-

heeee!"

"It's the witch!" shouted Rob.

"No," yelled Rick. "It's her *ghost!!!*"

"I *hate* evil space-witch ghosts!"

"I hunger!"

"She's comin' for us!"

"Let's get out of here!"

The boys scrambled out of the cellar. Craig and Rob immediately picked up their bikes. Rick ran over to the nearby clothes line.

"Hold on a second!" he shouted as he ran. "I have an idea!"

"Hurry!"

Rick yanked three of the spring loaded clothes pins off the line, and ran back to friends. As he did so, he pulled his pack of *The Dukes of Hazard* trading cards out of his back pocket.

"Take these! Clip them on your bike frames, so the cards are in your spokes. If you put cards in your spokes, it makes you go faster! Everyone knows that!"

"Right!" agreed Rob.

The boys deftly attached the cards, and hopped on their seats. Rick looked down into the cellar and saw the Ghost Witch rise up out of the well. He called to her.

"Hey! Up here you idiot!"

The Ghost Witch pointed at the boys and bellowed maniacally:

"I'll swallow you whole!"

"Follow me!" Rick ordered, and rode off on his bike, the other two boys followed him, the trading cards whirring in their spokes as they pedaled.

TLtltltltltltltltltltltl.

TLtltltltltltltltltltltl.

TLtltltltltltltltltltltl.

The Ghost Witch flew up out of the cellar door, and chased after them!

"There is no escape!"

With unearthly speed, the boys rode around to the front yard, passed Sherriff Wilson, and headed south down Old Mill Rd. The ghost rocketed through the air after them.

"What in the world is that?!" shouted Deputy Reynolds.

"I don't know," the Sherriff replied. "Greg, go check out the house and see if anyone in it needs help, or knows what's going on. I'll try the radio!"

"Right!" he said, running to the front door.

The Sherriff opened the door to his car, and tried the ignition. Nothing. He tried again. Still nothing. Miraculously, the car started on the third try. The Sherriff then put it into gear and headed down the road in pursuit of the apparition. He picked up the radio handset.

"Marcy, this is Josh! Marcy, this is Josh! Do you read me? Over."

"Read you loud and clear, Sherriff!"

"I want you to send another patrol car over to the corner of Spring and Old Mill Rd. Send an ambulance also. Over."

"Will do! Sherriff, we're starting to get reports of trouble over at the Town Square. Over."

"I'm headed that way now. Over."

6:59pm – Old Mill Rd.

TLtltltltltltltltltltltl.

The boys burned down the road, the screaming ghost hot on their heels.

"Old Mill only goes as far as Elm St!" Rick shouted. "When we get to Harvest, take a right into the Town Square, then head back south down Main!"

"What are we doing?" Craig asked.

"I can't say!"

"Why not?"

"I don't want her to hear!"

TLtltltltltltltltltltltl.

Rob glanced back over his shoulder.

"I think she's gainin' on us!"

"Run, fools! Run!"

"I *know* she's gaining on us!"

7:04pm – Town Square.

The townsfolk were shocked when Rick, Rob, and Craig came zipping through the square on their bikes like greased lightning.

"Outta the way! Outta the way!" yelled Rob

"Coming through!" yelled Craig.

TLtltltltltltltltltltltltl.

They were even more shocked when the cackling ghost of an evil space witch roared past them, in hot pursuit of the kids.

"Your Child Magic will be mine!"

Amanda Hanson screamed at the sight of the apparition.

Debbie Chambers grabbed her husband's arm.

"That was Craig, and the other boys! What was that thing after them?""

"I don't know!" Carlton replied.

The Sherriff's patrol car rolled into the square, he had his hazard lights flashing, as the cherry lights were visibly busted. He honked his horn repeatedly to get people to clear the way.

"We need to go after them!" said Jeff.

"Right, everyone get in the car!"

The four parents piled in to the car. Jeff switched on the ignition, and drove after the kids, with the accelerator pressed to the floor.

7:09PM – Main St.

TLtItItItItItItItItItItItI.

"We're almost there!" said Rick.

"You're end is near!"

TLtItItItItItItItItItItItI.

"Almost where?"

TLtItItItItItItItItItItItI.

"When we get to it, take the old dirt road to the creek!"

TLtItItItItItItItItItItItI.

"Why?"

"Trust me!"

TLtItItItItItItItItItItItI.

7:12pm – Grover Creek

The boys pedaled down the dirt road toward the creek. The Ghost Witch followed right behind them. Behind her was the Sherriff's car, followed by the parents.

TLtItItItItItItItItItItItI.

Rick called to his friends.

"Over to the ramp! Jump the creek! Jump the creek!"

"What?!"

"Just do it!"

"But we can't make it!"

"We can!"

The Ghost Witch inched closer to them. A vengeful fire burned in her eyes. She raised her vaporous arms in the air, poised to swing down upon the trio as soon as she was within range.

"Eeeeh-hee-hee-hee-hee-heeee!"

In his car, Sherriff Wilson contacted dispatch again.

"Marcy, this is Josh. I'm going to need another car, and another ambulance at Grover Creek, down the dirt road off Main. Make it quick! Over."

"Will do. Over."

One car back, the parents were panicking. Dirt was being kicked up all around them, and the car was shaking on the rough road.

"Why did they come down this way?" asked Amanda.

"We're going to run out of road." said Jeff. "It ends just up ahead, and then there's a hill that leads down to the creek."

"What are we going to do?"

"I don't know."

The boys rode past the end of the road, and headed straight down the hill towards the creek. The ghost was relentless in its pursuit.

"Just remember one thing!" shouted Rick.

TLtltltltltltltltltltltl.

The Sherriff saw the end of the road, applied the car brakes and slid to a halt, just before reaching the hill. He pushed his door open, and started to run down the hill.

"Just one thing!" repeated Rick.

TLtltltltltltltltltltltl.

Jeff Hanson saw the Sherriff's car come to a sudden halt. He slammed on the brakes, and turned the wheel in order to miss the squad car. The vehicle came to rest next to the Sherriff's.

The four parents rushed out of the car, and followed the Sherriff down the hill.

"When we jump the ramp, just remember…"

TLtltltltltltltltltltltl.

The decline ended, and the ground leveled out below the boys. They were about to hit the ramp. The ghost was closer than ever, about to strike.

"… keep pedaling!!" Rick yelled.

TLtltltltltltltltltltltl.

"Yee-haw!"

Rick jumped the ramp.

He kept pedaling.

"Yahoo!"

Craig jumped the ramp.

He kept pedaling.

"Mommyyyyyy!"

Rob jumped the ramp.

He kept pedaling.

As he ran down the hill, Jeff Hanson swore he saw blue and white lightning crackle through the spokes of the boy's tires.

The boys soared across the creek. It was as if their bikes were somehow riding on top of the air itself. Their metal frames glistened in the moonlight, and cast beautiful reflections in the shimmering water below them.

Rick touched down on the other side of the creek. Followed by Craig, then Rob.

"Hit the brakes! Hit the brakes!" Rick shouted.

All the boys slammed on their brakes and spun their bikes to a stop.

Debbie Chambers screamed when they did.

"Noooooo!"

The Ghost Witch launched itself over the ramp toward the boys. Its mouth enlarging to swallow them all whole.

"Now, you are mi.."

SPLA-

DOOOOOOOOM!

With a thunderous sound, the witch exploded in the middle of the air, in a ball of spectral fire and unearthly wind. All those watching it had to shield their eyes from the brightness of the ghostly fire. It was a tremendous blast that caused Carlton Chambers to almost lose his balance. The force blew the plank the boys used as a ramp over, and bent back plants.

Then, all the fire and wind, collapsed in upon itself, as if being sucked back into the ethereal void from where it came, and vanished without a trace.

The boys collapsed from exhaustion. They laid in the grass on their backs staring at the clear sky. They could hear their parents approaching, calling for them. After a moment Craig caught his breath.

"Hey Rick, how did you know that would happen?"

"I read in *Dracula*," he answered, panting, "that vampires, ghosts, and other evil things, can't cross running water."

"Really?" asked Rob.

"Really. It destroys them."

"I didn't know that," said Craig.

"That's funny," said Rick. "I mean, *everyone* knows *that*."

All three laughed as one.

7:45pm – Grover Creek

The red lights of the ambulance swirled across the waters, giving the creek a surprisingly inviting glow. The officers from the additional squad cars were busy taking statements, and signing forms. Sherriff Wilson was directing Deputy Reynolds to have the whole area taped off when Matt Davenport approached them.

"Thank you again for bringing me down here, Greg."

"No problem, Mr. Davenport," the Deputy replied. "But before you go anywhere, I want you to have one of these paramedics look at that head injury."

"I will," he said. "Josh, I also wanted to thank you for racing down here like you did to try to save my boy."

"I was happy to Mr. Davenport. Truth be told though, it was your boy, and the other kids, that did all the saving."

"Yes, they did." Matt beamed with pride. "How are you going to report all this to the higher-ups?"

"I've already been told the Governor is sending someone to investigate the whole thing."

"I wouldn't want to be in his shoes."

"Me either." Sherriff Wilson smiled.

Matt Davenport walked over to his grandson, and wrapped him in a wool blanket. He knelt down, and looked Rick in the eyes.

"Rick, I want to apologize to you. I should have known from the start that you wouldn't be involved in any troublemaking. I should have also known you wouldn't lie to me."

"It's ok, Grandpa Matt. After all, in the end you really did believe me. If you hadn't, you wouldn't have checked up on Billy."

"I suppose you're right about that."

"I'm just glad you're alright, grandpa."

"You're a good boy, Rick."

Rick smiled at his grandfather.

"I had a good teacher."

Jeff and Amanda Hanson stood beside their son as he overlooked the creek. Jeff put his hand on Rob's shoulder.

"I can't believe I jumped it."

"It was something to see, son."

"Maybe I should become a daredevil when I grow up."

"I won't stop you," said Jeff.

"I will!" said Amanda.

"Mandy!"

"Well, it's dangerous."

"Mom, life is dangerous. You won't get anywhere in it, if you're not brave."

Jeff laughed and ran his fingers through Rob's hair.

"When did you get to be so smart?"

"Tonight."

"Craig. Your mother and I were talking, and we wanted you to know, that we're very proud of you."

"Thanks, dad."

"And we're sorry," Debbie added.

"When we were told you did all of those bad things, we were so concerned what everyone in town might think, it didn't even occur to us to take you at your word."

"We'll know better next time, Craig."

"Thanks, mom," Craig said. "Although, I do think there is something you can do to help make it up to me for *this* time."

"What's that?"

"Hold on a second."

Craig stepped away from his parents and called over to both Rick and Rob. The trio converged at the top of the hill, and got into a huddle. Their respective parents looked on in puzzlement.

After a moment of deliberation, the boys broke their huddle, and Craig raised his hands to get everyone's attention.

"Mom, Dad, Mr. Hanson, Mrs. Hanson, Mr. Davenport, the three of us talked it over, and considering the circumstances… we're all going to need bigger allowances."

… and they got just that.

The End

7:15PM EST – CALIFORNIA.

Two thousand six hundred twenty-five miles away…

Hedy

Agnes

Goodrich

SCREAMED!

Thank You For Reading:

BIBLY O'GRIM's

Hallow'eve™ Frights – Book 1

ALL THE KIDS LOVE THAT SCARY STUFF

Story By

Bibly O'Grim

Book By

Randy Moses

Copyright © 2015 Randy Moses

Please Join Us Again Next Time.

About The Authors

RANDY MOSES lives in Madison, AL with his beautiful wife Anna, their beloved daughter Amy.

While he is writing, Randy likes to drink root beer and listen to his favorite bands: *The Birthday Massacre,* and *Within Temptation*.

His favorite authors are: *Charles Dickens, Douglas Adams,* and *H.P. Lovecraft.* His favorite book is *A Christmas Carol.*

BIBLY O'GRIM lives… somewhere. Probably.

Little is currently known about the famed storyteller and prankster, outside of anecdotal sightings of him on Halloween. On that day, there are always varying reports of him from everywhere across the globe. From Tokyo to Killarney to Berlin to Atlanta, he has been seen singing, dancing, eating, and just making merry in general.

It is well known that Bibly will dress in a costume to secretly join other trick-or-treaters on Halloween. Often many candy givers are left wondering if the quiet child, hiding in the back of a group of kids, was in fact actually 'good ol' Bibly' in disguise.

It is a growing tradition, come Halloween Night, to leave a cup of strong hot tea out on your back porch, to see if Bibly will stop by for a sip. He can get quite thirsty at night, so don't be surprised if you find the tea gone in the morning, with a piece of candy, or two, left in its place…